Have Fun on your
trip to an amazing
land called
US..!

Ron Watt
4/2/02

DATELINE: UBI

Sea
of
Japan

Yellow

Sea

East

China

Sea

Dateline: Ubi

Ron Watt

✺

To Simona for all your strength, kindness and radiance.
With all my love.

✺

©2001 Airport Books LLC

ISBN: 0-9709632-0-3

Library of Congress Catalog Card Number: 2001090832

Layout by Francine Smith

Edited by Michelle E. Wotowiec

Cover Art by Fred Mozzy

Submit all requests for reprinting to:
Greenleaf Book Group LLC
660 Elmwood Point, Aurora, OH 44202

Published in the United States by
Greenleaf Book Group LLC, Cleveland, Ohio.

www.airportbooks.com

www.greenleafbookgroup.com

＊

The fictional characters in this book are simply that. Any resemblance to any person living or dead is purely coincidental, by name or description. The real people, of course, are real.

＊

Dateline: Ubi (OO-Bee)

Table of Contents

CHAPTER ONE

The Simple, The Good,
The Bad

Not many men have a whole country named after them. Then, of course, few men have the ability to name a country after themselves. One would think this to be an egoist's predilection but not so with Ubi Ubi, who 24 years ago discovered a plot of land about 24 miles square at the southern tip of China on the Yellow Sea, across from Dalian. The land had been owned by the Catholic Church for more than 200 years but had been eventually deemed expendable. Ubi was able to purchase the land for just under $500,000 on time payments over 20 years. His days of traveling through Europe, China and the former Soviet Union were to come to an end.

Ubi Ubi, part Mongol, part Irish and another part Lithuanian, would have been considered a gypsy by many before he founded his small but verdant country a quarter of a century ago. He was not a gypsy but more of a nomad. It was the nature of his family members before him to move every so many months from one place to another. His entire life from childhood into adulthood into middle age he continued to do so. When he turned 48, he suddenly stopped moving. That was when he made his first payment to the Catholic Church on the land that he had acquired – the monthly cost of which was $2541.22, including compounded interest of 8.5 percent.

What Ubi Ubi knew 24 years ago and the Catholic Church did not was that the indigenous eefer tree produces an ancient herb that was known by his family to cure anxiety. It was not the eefer tree itself that produced the herb but rather the wing–like nuts that spawned from it four times a year. Thus, the eefer tree did not have to be torn down to produce the herb. In fact, the eefer tree was known to live hundreds of years in its dense jungle–like atmosphere. And no land mass contained as many eefer trees as that to be found in the plot of land soon to be named Ubi. That was 24 years ago. And today there are even more eefer trees, trees that over time were found to cure many forms of anxiety, madness and depression, rashes, acute alcoholism, shingles and certain strains of yeast infections. Today, at age 72, Ubi Ubi is an abundantly rich man, as are his wife and only son. Many of his country's constituents are rich as well, because Ubi Ubi is an inherently democratic leader who believes so fully in sharing the fruits of success.

But Ubi Ubi has a problem. He is afraid his country is going to be taken over. The Catholic Church wants it back. And closing in from sheer avarice are Texas real estate interests and, even worse, the goliath global pharmaceutical firm, E.H. Meris, headquartered in Bern, Switzerland. The real estate interests, headed by Tommy "Smiley" Watkins of Kilgore, Texas, better known as home to the Kilgore Rangerettes baton twirlers, are menacing as well. Watkins and his interests want to build homes and championship golf courses on Ubi's land mass, the 24 square miles of which are shaped like a slice of pizza pie. They are thinking, too, that they can build high rises, hotels and condos, similar to the neo-modern structures on Cancun. Ubi would become a striking Riviera that would attract gamblers, prostitutes and other creeps, as Ubi Ubi saw it, from North Africa, Eastern Europe and possibly India, Turkey and Egypt.

No one exactly knows what the mysterious Meris company is trying to do for sure, but many men and a few women in dark blue suits have been populating the streets of Ubi and could be seen in extended meetings at the Ubi Marriott.

Just last month, Premier Ubi sought the help of former American President Hanover Simpson, noted especially for his humanitarianism. President Simpson visited with Ubi Ubi and declared forcefully that Ubi was the land of Ubians and clearly no one else. "We cannot stand by as Ubi is mercilessly plundered by special private interests," Simpson told Ted Koppel on Nightline.

"What more can a non-sitting President of the United States do but stand by," asked Koppel. "Simply put, what can you do, sir?"

"I will do all it takes to save Ubi for the Ubians. Their eefer trees are theirs and theirs alone. I recommend that the United States take military action, much the same way we defended the Falkland Islands 15 years ago."

"Mr. President what exactly do you recommend?"

"We should go in with the big tanks, the Navy, air support and anything else it will take to ward off the enemy, Mr. Koppel."

"Mr. President, pardon my asking and in all due respect to you and your career as President, don't you find it somewhat conflicting that two parties who were heavy supporters of your campaign financing are now called the enemy? Seriously, how can you sit there or stand there or whatever you do and say that E.H. Meris Pharmaceuticals of North America, the unit of the Swiss company, and Smiley Watkins and his gang are the enemy when you took so much money from them for your campaigns for the Senate and the Presidency. As a matter of fact, Mr. President, my associates and I can track back to your days as mayor of Kilgore, Texas, and prove that Smiley Watkins financed your campaign. And I'm not even getting into what you and Smiley are reported to have done with the Kilgore Rangerettes."

In the traditional gesture of friendship, Ubi Ubi walked up to Jimmy Christian and crossed his arms. Jimmy crossed his in return. The shaking of hands is considered déclassé in Ubi and certainly unhealthful.

Jimmy was at his usual post, behind the vast mahogany bar of O'Fabo's. A thickly set black American, at 62, Jimmy still had the athletic look of the baseball star he was in the distant past. He was made to look all the younger with a black dye on his course head of hair. The dye was yet another product of the eefer tree.

In the mid-1960s, Jimmy was a thunderous home run hitter in the International League. Playing for the Toledo Mud Hens, he once hit a 550-foot home run out of the Lucas County Rec Center ballpark that broke the windshield of Alan Saunders' Rolls Royce. Saunders was the creator of the fabled comic strips Steve Roper and Mary Worth and was worth a bundle. Saunders felt so bad that Jimmy felt so bad about the incident that, after the car was fixed, he let Jimmy drive it around for 10 days during a home stand. Jimmy thought then that he would never ever drive a Rolls Royce again. He was right.

Jimmy and his pal, Ike Brown, got called up to the Detroit Tigers for several seasons during the late 1960s and early 1970s. Neither really made it full time, for that was when the Tigers were invincible, winning the World Series in seven games in 1968. No one was going to knock Kaline, Horton and Northrup out of the outfield.

Jimmy bounced around the International League for the next several years and that was it for his career. He knows today that had he been born thirty years later, he'd be making a couple million bucks a year, if not more. That's what they pay guys with .258 batting averages who can hit 35 homers and knock in 100 runs. He knows that a lot of guys who are in the swelled majors today might not have made it to triple-A when he was playing.

With his chunky, six-foot frame, Jimmy still looks like a tough dude. But he has the joyful countenance of a zen master. Jimmy leaned his beefy arms over the bar and greeted Ubi Ubi.

"Ubi, you have done so much for this country. You deserve to be at peace. You ain't at peace any more. You are the man... the man of the people. But you can't find no sense in what is happenin' these days."

"Jimmy, a long time ago I did that deal with Cardinal Reidy. Finbar Reidy. He thought he took me to the cleaners for $500,000 for this land. But in a few years it was apparent that I was the one who had won. And our people, they had won too. The Church was so upset with these events – after we discovered the power of the eefer seeds – that the good Cardinal Reidy was demoted to the new posting of Royal Archbishop of Morani," said Ubi.

"Yeah, I remember. They fixed that prick real good," responded Jimmy Christian.

"Ha, ha," laughed Ubi Ubi. "They sent him to Morani, that little swampy island off the coast of Pakistan as some sort of missionary. The have locusts there the size of falcons. Now, if they could, they would send me there to replace him, to be like him, an ambassador to the lepers. After all these years, they, the Vatican lawyers, want all this back because they are saying I stole this land from them for a ridiculous price and Cardinal Reidy's paperwork is no good. They think I made enough money off this land and now it is their turn to have it back."

Jimmy breathed deeply as he poured Ubi a mohito, a rummy, lime and sugar infested cocktail that was mostly Captain Morgan's. In the background, Jimmy Buffet's cantata to relaxation, "Cheeseburger In Paradise," was playing softly over the P.A. system. As Ubi swilled the drink, Jimmy pondered. "We could start a war, bro, to keep the damn Vatican lawyers out of here. That'd make big news in America. Simpson could help us, like he helps everyone else. He was here. You had him here last month. He promised he would help settle this. What'd you think, boss?"

Ubi frowned, his five-foot-eight frame bent over the mahogany bar. Ubi was a handsome man, if not simply an exotic one with his mix of heritage. "He just acts like he will help. He'll not. He won't piss off the Catholic Church. And he'll try to screw us with Meris Pharmaceuticals or those oppressive Texas real estate guys. Whatever suits him best he'll do."

For a premier, Ubi Ubi had the habits of a simple man. He'd rather drink at O'Fabo's than down the street at the UBI Club, which was built in 1893, mainly for visiting Catholic wealth. For all his years of traveling, Ubi identified mostly with the common man. Some years ago he changed the name of the St. William Cloister to simply the UBI Club. He took out the skeet shoots, removed the boxing rings (where bare-knuckled priests would beat each other to bits as bishops watched) and took out the musty chairs and sofas of old for Herman Miller-designed furnishings. Still, he resented the pomp of the Club, preferring to mingle with Jimmy Christian and the denizens that filtered through O'Fabo, a bar that in the Ubian culture roughly means "Oh, Don't Worry." Shortly after landing in Ubi, 20 some years ago, Jimmy Christian was prompted to start the little bar, because there wasn't much action in the central Ubian area, known as Fung-Hi. Fung-Hi wasn't a city. It was really a neighborhood where all the business was done.

As Ubi downed his third mohito, he looked out the window of the small O'Fabo bar and grill, past the dark wooden chairs and tables and out toward a long white limousine. He recognized the visage of Smiley Watkins, as the chubby Texas real estate magnate alighted the car. Smiley Watkins looked like a man after a big steak – more ways than one.

❁

When Smiley Watkins strode through the Dutch door, Jimmy Christian sighed noticeably. Not many people make Jimmy Christian unhappy. This was an exception. Smiley

Watkins slammed his palm on the bar and asked for a Kettle One vodka on the rocks. Watkins didn't realize that two stools down from him was seated Ubi Ubi, the man who created this special nation, named after himself. The two men were similar in their toughness but dissimilar in every other way.

"Smiley Watkins, Kilgore, Texas," said Watkins to the bartender. "My first trip to Ubi and I'm here to make it productive. Want to get to know the right people and maybe you're one of them. What's your name?"

"Jimmy Christian. Been here a long time. It's a nice place with a lot of nice people. We're from all over the world. We like it peaceful. We're just peaceful people."

"Yeah, ya're peaceful all right. And most of ya are rich as hell, aren't ya? This place is like Kuwait, without the oil but with something else that makes a hell of a lot of money," Smiley snarled.

"If it wasn't for the man sittin' next to you on the right, there wouldn't be a Ubi," said Jimmy. "He figured it out for himself and he did all right by the rest of us, too."

"What'd your name, pardner?" Smiley asked the man next to him. "Ya been around here a long time, too?"

Jimmy Christian jumped in, "This here, my friend, is the premier of Ubi. This here is Ubi Ubi himself, the man who started this whole place."

"We'll, I'll be damned. I wanted to meet ya on this trip but I didn't think it would be that easy. What ya doing in this joint? I thought ya only stayed in yar Taj Mahal," said Smiley Watkins, lighting up an Indios presidente. "I recognize ya now from CNN. But ya look a lot smaller. Ya looked pretty big standing next to President Simpson," Watkins chortled. "Ya must have been standin' on an orange crate. What d'ya want to do with yar country? Yar're in yar seventies. This would be a good time to cash in, don't you think? What d'ya want to do?... shall I call ya premier or what? That's what Simpson calls ya on TV."

"Just call me Ubi," said the premier. "Just call me what everyone else does. As for our country, I only want it to continue, as is, a safe haven for good people who have good intentions. That's it. And what might be your intentions, Mr. Watkins? What could they be?"

"We're going to turn this dump into what Cuba was like in the 1950s," said Watkins. "And we're going to make ya so rich in the process that ya'll be living in Fiji, in a big manse with ten servants and a couple of concubines."

In the Ubi Marriott, six men and one female, dressed in blue suits, sat near the lobby waterfall. They were all registered under the company name, E.H. Meris. No one knows better than the oldest one in the group, 40-year-old Bobbe Birstein, what an industry coup they would have if they could take control of the eefer market. Birstein, a Swiss, is the international director of product development for Meris, a company whose origins can be traced back 153 years to an apothecary in Bern. Over those years the company gradually grew to be the largest and most powerful pharmaceutical company in the world.

Among the entourage with Birstein on this trip is Genston (Genny) Chancellor, a Yalie, who since having graduated in 1984 has worked his way through the company maze in America. He now is marketing manager for special lines at the firm's U.S. headquarters in Armonk, New York. His title might not seem to carry much weight on the surface but it means a lot in the Meris system because he is the guy handling the developing lines - in other words, he serves as the chief scout for products upon which the company will make its future billions. Tight-lipped and overly confident, Genny makes a sinister counterpart to the Swiss, Birstein.

With them was Sheryl Chan, a 27-year-old bio-chemist who serves as Chancellor's chief troubleshooter - and opportunist. Dark-haired, dressed in a dark blue Armani, creamy complexion, five-six, she looks like a supporting actress in the latest-version of Mission Impossible.

These are the key players in the Meris brigade invading Ubi. They should be wearing jungle fatigues. But they are dressed in blue – or grey, their home team colors.

"It's amazing that Ubi Ubi has been able to sell the eefer produce to the small chemical companies and has continued to avoid us," said Birstein, in almost impeccable English, except for a few naturally mispronounced "W"s. "Eefer has become too big for us to ignore. In essence, Ubi Ubi has placed his little fiefdom into an oligarchy. He virtually controls the product, because no other place on earth can propagate the eefer tree like Ubi can. Never in pharmaceutical history has their been a raw product that can cure so many ills."

"And we don't know how many more cures there are," evoked Genny Chancellor. "Even though eefer has been used in many products for a long time, the media hardly know about it, doctors hardly know about eefer, Andrew Weil has not even talked about eefer. We've got to seize this opportunity. It's the miracle drug of the 21st century. The companies licensed by Premier Ubi to process eefer could ultimately merge... there must be ten or twelve of them already. They could kill us. It's time we act."

"Relax, relax," responded Birstein. "Vee're the biggest and the best. Vee didn't get that vay by sitting on our haunches. Vee are Switzerland, all of Europe, the Far East, and America and vee are even parts of South America, the parts vee vant that is. It is just a matter of time. Just a matter of time. Vith our brainy trust, vee shall vin the battle for eefer. Eefer shall be ours and ours alone."

※

CHAPTER TWO

"New York, New York"

THE NEXT NIGHT, Smiley Watkins returned to O'Fabo's. He was in rare form. He had been drinking Beefeater martinis all afternoon at the Ubi Club.

It was about 8 p.m. and jazz pianist extraordinaire, Caz Caswell, and his able sidekick, Felonius Assault, were just getting warmed up with their hip rendition of the St. Louie Blues. These two are the last of a breed. Their music swings hard and you can understand the tunes they play. They weren't schooled at any fancy place of academe. Not at a place like, Berklee, in Boston, noted for producing, especially lately, musicians who are pyrotechnic but for some reason lack heart, soul or the ability to appease an audience. Caz likes to opine, "Hey, man, if you don't know the audience is part of the band, you can't know shit about music."

Caz Caswell is 74 years old. His real first name is Charles, which Jimmy Christian is prone to calling him. He wears a beret. He appears to be almost black but he is white. He is strong from years of beating the board, an instrument that is part of the percussive family, though many people don't know that. A lot of piano players have strong shoulders and forearms from the very physical nature of the instrument.

Felonius Assault is 66. The jazz world likes to peg hip juxtapositions of first and last names on its people. His real first name is Densmore, but everybody for years has called him Felonius, maybe because it sounded good against his last name and maybe because of his feisty personality. His last name is derived from his French Moroccan blood on his father's side. The word in French would be pronounced "Azz-Sew," but in English it's just like it looks, "Assault." He is mostly black and he is a disciple of the great bassist Ray Brown, playing as best he can those fat, lustrous chords of Brown's.

Caswell and Assault together make good noise. In fact, the sound blends together so well that it is as one. As good as Caswell is, he isn't as good as when he is playing with Assault. And they have been doing so for a quarter century, having met at Ronnie Scott's jazz club in London in the mid-seventies. They started touring together and essentially played 'round the world, from Johannesburg to Osaka to Melbourne to New York to Montreal to L.A. to Paris, Brussels and Milano. One of their favorite places was "The Senator" in Toronto. There they were booked for two weeks, two shows a night, always sold out. They'd make "seven and seven." They'd take "the door," instead of a performance fee and would clear a good $7000 each week. In between the longer gigs they'd take two-nighters at places like "Nighttown" in Cleveland or "The Green Door" in Chicago.

Jimmy Christian, a fan of straight-ahead swingin' jazz, called their agent in 1988 to book the guys for two weeks. He thought they'd be perfect for his O'Fabo club. And, of couse, they were. They went back on the road after that, "makin' the rounds," came back to Ubi the next year and, you guessed it, never left.

Smiley Watkins, the real estate shark ambled over to the tiny rise of a bandstand and requested, "New York, New York," a piece of horrid music that all good jazz musicians truly and unadulteratedly hate. The boys had just completed a Sonny Rollins' take on "Fallin' In Love With Love" in the 4/4ths tempo in which he had made it famous, not in the original waltz tempo in which it was written. Wonderful. They got a nice recognition from the crowd of locals and visitors at Jimmy Christian's place.

"How 'bout playin' "New York, New York" you guys?" Smiley croaked, with the usual insensitivity of the jackass that he truly is. The guys looked at him quietly, not indicating their disdain for this peculiar type of person that had no concept of the spiritual aspects of the music. No sense of what the audience wanted to hear. No sense of the deep meaning of the tunes Caz and Felonius liked to play.

Smiley flung a $50 bill on the glistening black Yamaha and announced to all who could hear him, which was basically everyone in the 100-seat room, "That's my favorite song. My very favoritist song of all," pronounced Smiley, who then shuttled back to his stool. Jimmy Christian, behind the bar, snorted. The guys played "New York, New York." Thank God Smiley or anyone else did not try to sing along.

It is now 11:15 p.m. and Smiley is on, maybe, his 10th Dewar's and soda. Jimmy Christian is not happy.

In between slapping $50 bills on the piano and ordering more reprises of "New York, New York" from the band, Smiley was telling tall Texas tales at the bar. Often on a ballad, his voice could be heard over the music. The guys, being purely whimsical to themselves, were playing Antonio Carlos Jobim's beautiful Brazilian elegy, "How Insensitive." Some people in the crowd, unbeknownst to Smiley, snickered. Smiley was telling a woman and a man from America about his mentorship in politics under Lyndon Baines Johnson, which was a preposterous untruth. At 58, Smiley fashioned himself quite the raconteur, quite the sophisticate, but this foolish premise belied him. As he prattled, he would place his meaty palm on the woman's shoulder. Her companion who thought of Smiley only as an oaf looked away. Jimmy, whose visage was mostly a happy one, glowered.

This would be Smiley's fourth request for "New York, New York, this after the band had played, "Blue Monk," the signature Theolonius Monk piece, perhaps one of the best in the bop lexicon.

"One more time, one more for the good guy," Smiley commanded.

"Shit, shit, shit," responded Densmore Assault, at which point he placed down his bass, walked off the little stage and went directly for Smiley Watkins. With his large bassist's hands he grabbed for Smiley's chubby throat and squeezed until Smiley's rubicund face turned a higher level of crimson. "You little piece of Texas turd, I'm going to whip your fat ass," quaked Assault. "You little fake rich nothing blowhard, you A-hole dick!"

By now, Smiley Watkins was flat on his lardy back and Felonius Assault was living up to his name, punching and punching Watkins contorted face. The crowd, which first went quiet at the developments, started to cheer Felonius Assault, who had all the earmarks of Mike Tyson in one of those bouts where he wins in the first 50 seconds.

Jimmy Christian moved in to quell the battle and to essentially save Assault's big but talented hands. Jimmy picked up the little Texas tub by the back of his collar and the back of his belt and pushed him forward toward the vestibule of O'Fabo's and out the oaken door... all the while Caz Caswell was giving the crowd a harmonic improvisation of the song he most hated, "New York, New York."

On the brick walkway in front of O'Fabo's, Smiley sat on a small puddle. He had watered his shorts.

❁

CHAPTER THREE

The Chief Of Staff

PREMIER UBI UBI was at the official residence having his favorite breakfast dish of cornmeal streusel with wild Maine blueberries. His wife, Taki, was on the phone, as was her custom in the early morning. She was talking long distance to her sister in Punta Arenas, Chile, Taki's hometown. They were talking about a much-needed holiday to the home country and her urging of her husband to come with her. Ubi Ubi had often been too busy to accompany her on such a journey far away from his responsibilities as leader of the Ubians.

Taki felt it imperative that her husband have some time off from the pressures he was encountering of late and wished that he would go with her for a fortnight of the calming influences of Punta Arenas.

"I'm not ready to go," said Ubi. "Our people are prepared to revolt against the recent oppression we are experiencing from three different sides, the worst of which I don't know. It would be a bad time for me to leave our country."

"We should go, we should go," said Taki, putting the phone on the receiver. "It will be good for you to get away from all this. You'll be fresher and more able when you get back. We need to spend some time together. You haven't been to Punta Arenas in years."

Taki, whose full name is Takita Salernas del Rios-Ubi, is petite and dark, with fine features. Her hair remains jet black (she has some Inca bloodstreams in her Chilean background) and she still has the figure of a woman much younger than her 56 years. In 1964 she had been the fourth runner-up in the Miss Universe contest, having earlier been Miss Chile. In the performance category she played the Spanish guitar and then did a little Flamenco dance with her tap shoes. Her radiance is still to this day with her. She and Ubi are a good pair, she the quieter and more serious, he the more gregarious and the bit of a cutup.

They have one son, the 25-year-old Shif-Lee Ubi, today at his young age the Minister of the Interior for the country of Ubi. Not an easy job or one solely given out of pure nepotism. "He worked long and hard in the eefer forests, even as a pre-adolescent," Ubi has often said. "Today, he is integral to the growth of our national product, a product that provides work and money for many of the 60,000 Ubians."

While Ubi Ubi pondered Taki's pleadings for a mutual holiday, the "business" phone suddenly rang. On the line was Admiral Robert Peter Schnuck, Ubi's chief of staff and his operations officer of sorts. Participating in the conference call with Admiral Schnuck was the Ubian information officer, Artha Crowder. The two of them are not exactly the likes of Leon Panetta and Michael McCurry but they are not just loyal fools either. Ubi counted on them as his key aides, along with Shif-Lee and, of course, Taki. In a country as small as Ubi, the group really could not do any material damage, and, overall, they were quite effective in their curious way.

Admiral Schnuck spoke first and with a laconic sense of urgency.

"Ubi, we've got people coming at us in three different ways and they are not being at all nice about it," Admiral Schnuck entoned. "These lawyers from the Holy See are driving me bonkers, the idiot from Texas is throwing a lot of big money around trying to buy us out and turn our land into a miniature Cancun, and maybe the worst group of all, those reprobates from E.H. Meris, are accusing us of illegally shipping eefer seeds into market without the proper sanctions from the World Health Organization. I'm somewhat at the end of my rope with all this, and Artha is going schizoid on me with all the pressure. He's getting very persnickety."

"I am not, I am nottttt!" said the other voice in the phone meeting. "I just can't take all this agitation at once. It used to be pleasant around here. I can't handle all these media people, government officials from other governments and the handlers for E.H. Meris, Smiley Watkins, and the goddamned Church," Artha sputtered. "Robert and I have absolutely no idea about what to do next. Nobody is listening to us or taking our point of view. What d'ya think, boss? Suggestions, suggestions, we need suggestions!"

Ubi Ubi yearned for his right arms to take more decisive responsibility, rather than continuously require him to come up with answers, but he was never one to show his annoyance and he genuinely liked Admiral Schnuck and Artha Crowder and he appreciated their earnest allegiance to him and the country.

"Settle down, settle down gentlemen," said Ubi. "I assure you we will get through these waves of anguish.

"Always remember our country was just a patch of eefer trees 25 years ago. We built it from that and made it a country of envy for many other nations. It is the strength of our land, our people and our eefers that will bring these self-seeking affronts against us to a resolve. And I believe all good countries in the world will be on our side as we wage war against the agendas of oppression."

"Ubi, you are not suggesting that we go to war over this are you?" asked Admiral Schnuck. "We have always been peaceable people. We don't even have munitions, not even one submarine or one tank."

"Aha, Admiral Schnuck, I am not suggesting a war sort of war. Oh, no, not at all. I'm in favor of a war of words, a war of influence, a war of guilt, a war of national pride, a war utilizing the international media to state our plight and win the support of all other good countries," Premier Ubi stated quietly.

Admiral Schnuck, who had risen through the ranks of the British Navy and who was one of the leaders of the invasion of the Falkland Islands in the tidy little war with Argentina a couple of decades ago, has a pinched-nez visage. A squat man of some six-feet in height, he has the look of a smaller version of the late General DeGaulle of France. He has a beak on him that is smaller than the late De Gaulle's but it is prominent as it juts out from his wire-framed glasses. He is not an overly active man. He prefers long, leisurely lunches over cocktails and steak and then a long afternoon nap in his office to prepare for early cocktail hour.

Artha Crowder, on the other hand, is wiry, worrisome and often out of sorts. He is taller than Admiral Schnuck and much thinner. His hair is tied in a bun in back of his head, though on top of his head he is completely bald, save a strand or two of blond-gray. He and Admiral Schnuck work well together, though they really aren't good friends. Their commonality is that they both adore Premier Ubi Ubi and they love what the country of UBI stands for, although it doesn't have a constitution, a bill of rights, or any working lawyers.

"This approach you have to war, Ubi, is going to put much pressure on me and my office," Artha said. "I have just one secretary and two interns, one from Canada and the other from the States. They don't know that much."

"Artha, my friend, I assure you that you can direct this information challenge," said Ubi. "You are one of the best information ministers in the world. You must believe in yourself more. At any rate, Admiral Schnuck, you and I will form a triumvirate that will encourage all good people from all good countries to side with our plight, people who will help us win the war of words and fight off the enemies who would take our land and livelihood from our people.

"And very importantly, I will ask Shif-Lee to ensure that our 60,000 people, even those less fortunate in the middle-class barrios of Fung-Hi, understand that as peaceable people, we will not act in traditional war but within the war of public opinion," Premier Ubi continued. "We are already doing that, as witnessed by the recent visit of Hanover Simpson. He is the first former president of the United States to visit our country. I believe he will try to help us, even though he might exploit our situation.

"Let us meet for drinks tonight at O'Fabo's and we can discuss our strategy in further detail," Ubi told his two comrades.

CHAPTER FOUR

The Confused Plastic Key

SHERYL CHAN OPENED THE DOOR to her room at the Ubi Marriott, with Genny Chancellor right behind her. It was shortly past midnight. They had spent the evening at O'Fabo's, listening to Caz Caswell and Felonius Assault and were still reeling with laughter at the events that occurred there.

Right after the fat Texan with the pale blue eyes had requested "New York, New York," just after he had been rubbing Sheryl's behind at the bar, the bassist in the band lurched off the stage and started pummeling the fat man. It happened so quickly that neither Sheryl nor Genny quite conceived what was going on. One minute this pug with the Texas drawl was sloppily groping Sheryl and the next second he was on his back getting his nose bopped over and over. He offered no contest to the large black man who had just before been playing sweet music.

As for the groping, neither Sheryl nor Genny took it too seriously. The fat guy was about 30 years older than they were and, at this point in the night, totally out of his mind. He was harmless though annoying as hell.

Sheryl and Genny sat down on the sofa in her junior suite and turned on CNN, about the only way you could have contact with the larger world from Ubi. Sheryl and Genny had worked together at E.H. Meris in the states for more than a year. They were friends but there seemed the likelihood of more than that. They weren't intimate yet, but being together so much in their travels and back at the home fort in Armonk, New York, they sometimes would get a little horny and would eat some face, just as if it were like another martini. They did so while watching Larry King, who was interviewing the Dahli Lama, who in turn was having difficulty understanding Larry's questions but did a good job of smiling and nodding. The Dahli's smiling and nodding had a sedative effect on Sheryl and Genny, who started nodding themselves. A noticeably perplexed Larry King looked to the side, apparently toward his staffers off screen, as if his people and the Dahli's people hadn't quite understood the nature of tonight's interview, which in essence seemed to be about the Dahli's new book. King, though, plowed right through as the Dahli smiled and occasionally said something profound and understandable.

Sheryl nudged Genny and the Yalie awoke by doing something most un-Yalie, farting, not once but twice. This could be one of the reasons that their relationship hadn't raced forward any farther.

Now at the door, Sheryl gave Genny a quick peck goodnight, at which point he farted again. Sheryl closed the door to suite 1617, while Genny farted once more as he left the alcove entering the main corridor.

❈

About a half hour later, Tommy "Smiley" Watkins decided to leave the downstairs bar at the Marriott, where he finished off his favorite cognac, Hine, and headed to his two-bedroom suite. After leaving O'Fabo's earlier in the evening, he had gone back to his suite, passed out, got up, took a shower and put on some new duds. He was ready to party some more, despite the humility of being thrown out of O'Fabo's, wetting his pants and generally making an ass of himself. He was ready to go.

After inhaling three Hines, Smiley was told the lobby bar was closing. Knowing he had no alternative but to go back to his suite, he reached for his plastic key card, but it wasn't to be found in his pocket. Smiley wobbled over to the reception desk and asked the clerk for another key. She obligingly secured one for him and he headed for the elevators.

A little disoriented, Smiley held the bottle of Hine, which he had bought from the bartender for another nightcap or two, under his left arm. Fiddling with the key with his right hand, he opened the door to suite 1617 and stumbled in. He walked into the bedroom to take off his clothes, turned on the bed light and realized there was a sleeping, beautiful young woman with dark hair in his bed.

❋

CHAPTER FIVE

Lawyers Are Lawyers

IT WAS 4 P.M. THE NEXT DAY and Admiral Schnuck and Artha Crowder were waiting as Premier Ubi Ubi walked into O'Fabo's. The Admiral's favorite drink is a Beefeater on the rocks, two olives. Crowder, who had a bad stomach, was nursing a pinot grigio, which he really did not prefer to have. But he felt he had to be one of the guys.

Jimmy Christian knew that you could never tell what the Premier was going to have to drink. Ubi switched off. Two days ago it was mohitos, yesterday vodka chilled, today it would be French 75s. Jimmy poured the first.

"Ube, you'll never believe what happened here last night," said Jimmy. "That fat little shithead from Texas got himself into a fight with Densmore and I thought Dens was going to kill him. He would have killed him, if I hadn't picked them apart and thrown that Texas turd breath out the door."

Ubi just shook his head and laughed. "We have always been known as a nation of peaceable people," Premier Ubi said. "But these days it seems everything is having an edge to it. This is not what this country stands for."

"You are right, Ube. You are so right," Jimmy answered. "How's your French 75?"

"It is good, real good after a long day," said Ubi. "But I am sure my day wasn't as long as that of my colleagues here who this morning had a meeting with the lawyers from the Holy See. I can't wait to hear about that one."

"Ubi, Ubi, I thought Artha here was going to have the big one, and he is even a Catholic," said Admiral Robert Peter Scnuck. "We have no edge way. On every point there is no flexibility, no negotiation. Their way or the highway."

"But Admiral Schnuck you know we have a perfectally sound and fully paid off mortgage with the Catholic Church. It was signed by Cardinal Finbar Reidy and me 24 years ago. It was fully notarized and titled, financed through the Bank of the Holy See for $500,000 and it is no longer a loan, because we paid it off this past year," exclaimed Ubi Ubi. "What is there to worry about?"

"The lawyers from the Holy See say you stole the land for $500,000, when it is worth perhaps a hundred times that," answered Admiral Schnuck. "And they say the eefer tree production brings in billions of dollars a year and will bring much more as the scientific world understands more about the miracles of the eefer seed. In a nutshell, they want their piece of the action or they want the land back. They would work out a settlement, but it is no where near in our favor."

"Admiral Schnuck, lest I remind you, you are more than a decorated British naval officer of the highest standing, you are also a respected attorney," said Ubi. "You are their match."

"Look, my dear friend and leader, in all due respect, nobody is a match for the real estate acumen of these lawyers. Afterall, they are from the Catholic Church," said the Admiral.

"Then we'll appeal to the Pope, and we'll use Hanover Simpson, the former President of the United States of America, to help us. This is patently unfair and it affects 60,000 Ubians," said Ubi.

"Premier, I have made calls to Simpson's people," chimed in Artha Crowder, the Ubian information minister. "They are telling me he is in meetings the next two weeks at the Bel Air Hotel in California. He's working on two movie deals, one for TV and one for the big screen and cannot be bothered, though I was thinking he might take a call from you directly, Ubi. That might be a good idea. It might even be a good idea for you to see him personally."

"Well we should do whatever is necessary to make our point and get ourselves extricated from this mess," said Ubi. "Taki has been bugging me about taking a holiday in Chile very soon. Perhaps we could fly to Los Angeles on the way."

"I wish those lawyers from the Holy See would stop in here," said Jimmy Christian. "I'd poison their drinks.

"They'd never stop in here, though, 'cause they're too haughty," he continued. "They have to hang at the Ubi Club."

"You think this is something, wait till you hear about the meeting we had this afternoon with the representatives from E.H. Meris, the pharmaceutical company," said Artha Crowder. "They make the Vatican lawyers seem like our long lost friends."

"Yes, Ubi, these thieves really want to buy our land and throw us out and if we don't take the buyout they'll run us out. They are the largest privately held drug company on earth and they don't like the fact that we deal with 12 smaller pharmaceutical firms in the production of eefer. They know that there is considerable money to be made in the years ahead with the miracle of eefer, an herb the likes of which have never been seen in the modern world for the cure of so many common ills. They want to take it over and license the product," the Admiral explained.

"But that is what we have been doing for the past decades," said Ubi. "We have licensed eefer to our 12 partner companies and we have kept prices down for all concerned - especially the consumer end-users. Meris would ruin these relationships and send prices skyrocketing."

"Yes," answered Admiral Schnuck. "If Meris can get this land it will turn it into an eefer plantation, run the population out, grow more eefer trees and control all eefer production. Oh, it will be happy to license eefer to others, even our 12 smaller partners. But that price will be too high for the partners to be competitive. They'll go out of business and we will be left without our country. They're willing to pay you a tremendous price for the land. You could live in splendor somewhere else but there would be no more country called Ubi."

"First and foremost, I am not going to give up this land just to make a lot of money. I have plenty already," said Ubi. Eefer has been very good to my family and me. But in good conscience I cannot be involved with something that would displace 60,000 other Ubians. Avarice was not the basis upon which our country was built."

"And later this week, we have to deal with another predator, Smiley Watkins," again chimed in Artha Crowder. "He's already made quite a notice for himself in town with his partying. But when he's sober, he's tough as nails. He's got a whole phalanx of his understudies and co-investors arriving on Friday and they want to buy our land as well. They don't care about the eefer trees; they are interested in gambling casinos, shore development, golf courses, condos and big hotels. They don't care about the fact that billions can be made from eefer trees, because they know they can make billions off the business they know so well - commercial real estate. Watkins says he'd keep some eefer trees for adornment and for some pocket money but all he really cares about is real estate."

"We have our work cut out for us, but I think we can win these battles, especially in the court of world opinion," Ubi concluded. "Watkins really isn't too smart; he can find other areas of the world to develop in his manner, like the shores of Croatia, even Iceland. If he could look beyond his nose, he might see that the true value of our land is the eefer, the value of which cannot be calculated. But he is insensitive and uncaring for anything but his obvious intentions.

"The Holy See lawyers," he continued, "are no different from other lawyers. Essentially they are with a firm, the Church. They run in droves, seniors and lackies, one lawyer more boring than the next. They are thuggish, impertinent and self-minded, like most lawyers. If we back off, they'll run over us; if we push forward, they, like most bullies, will capitulate, especially with a world of force behind us.

"As for E.H. Meris, we will have our hands full. They are rich and exude power. What they see is theirs. Like our other two oppressors, they lack a human conscience. They may be more sinister than the other two, though all in the name of the good of science and the wellbeing of consumers. They will use all their global communications, political and legal resources to thwart us. But I think, if we're smart, we'll be appeasing to public opinion because we are David and they Goliath.

"This is more than simply the difference between good and evil, right and wrong. This is our land and it is our land rightly and squarely and, even though we don't have a constitution and a bill of rights, because we do not have any indigenous lawyers in Ubi and don't want them here, we must protect the interests of our people to the hilt.

"But beyond everything else, the true purpose of our land is to provide a place that is not contentious for those living here. That is serene, happy and beautiful. This is why I settled here and created Ubi. And that, my friends, is what we seek to protect at all cost. I know we can do it."

As so often, it was Ubi, not his advisors, who could see beyond the trouble and he knew what corrective action to take.

CHAPTER SIX

A Feather in the Nest

LATE THE PREVIOUS NIGHT, Sheryl Chan was awaken to a commotion in her suite, 1617. When Smiley Watkins had lost his plastic key card and had gone to the desk to get a new one, the clerk had made a mistake, or, more likely, Smiley had given her the wrong room number. In any event, he opened suite 1617, instead of his own, across the alcove, 1619.

The woman in the bed that he thought was his bed was Sheryl Chan. The smell of booze and the heavy thump on the bed woke Sheryl up. In a jolt, she recognized Smiley Watkins and retreated, her naked body covered by pulled up sheets. She could only think the worst, but she could not scream.

The last words out of Smiley's mouth before he passed out were, "Lookie, lookie here, ol' Smiley gonna have hisself some fun to-night!" As he sloped down, he fell on top of Sheryl. In a paean to romance, he feebly warbled, "I knew I could score ya . . . . . . against that, dumb, dub-ass, dumb-ass, dick, dickhead . . . ya were with . . . at OOOOooooo'Fabooooo's . . . . . ."

Sheryl pulled herself out from under Smiley and fell on the floor. She was shaking and confused as she rang the front desk for the security people. They seemed to take an inordinate time to get to her suite. She was quite a sight but with her natural Euro-Asian-American beauty, her dark hair and black eyes and perfect complexion, she was certainly not the kind of woman who would be in a bedroom with Smiley Watkins, no matter how wealthy he is.

Sheryl is the polar opposite of the red-neck, get lucky, get rich 58-year-old Smiley. Her father, of Japanese descent, is a research scientist at Washington University in St. Louis. Her mother, a Romanian/Austrian, is a violist in the St. Louis Symphony and before that had been with the Vienna Philharmonic, perhaps the best orchestra in the world. She decided to follow her husband's career, however, and move with him to the States, where he was given the Ferrbeurger chair in bio-genetic science at Johns Hopkins and latter went on to St. Louis to study bio-materials and bio-medicine at WashU.

They still live in a small but quaint three-bedroom house in the exclusive suburb of LaDue, notably the home of many of St. Louis's old-line royalty and some of the town's top corporate executives.

Sheryl is anything but a spoiled brat, however. Her parents are of the old world. They believe in musical and scientific education. They love all forms of culture. And they brought these values to her. She somehow had inherited her father's love for science and her mother's talents in music. Sheryl had the ability to be a classical pianist, if she had chosen that course. She was that good. When it came time to go to college she chose, with her parents' blessing, a dual major in music and biology at Case Western Reserve University in Cleveland. She would attend the Cleveland Institute of Music, one of the five best such conservatories in the country, to major in piano, and she would take a second major in bio-sciences at Case.

Sheryl's outgoing personality led her in other directions upon graduating from college. Besides being gorgeous in the most exotic way, she had an affinity for sales. And people realized that immediately. They could see that she was natural with people and genuinely enjoyed being with them. She was self-possessed in the best ways possible.

When E. H. Meris was interviewing on campus for its U.S. operations, with the chance of overseas assignments, their representatives immediately were attracted to Sheryl. They offered her a job at $30,000 starting pay plus commission to go into their extensive training program. She was placed in the Midwest marketing section of the company and did well from the start. They had her pegged for the marketing group at the company's American headquarters in Armonk, New York, and she arrived there by the time she was 25, already making $60,000 per year on the road and next moving into a post that paid $75,000 plus bonuses.

Today, at 28, she is one of the fast-rising female stars of the company, with the title of vice president-developmental sales. Her base salary is $150,000 and she is a key figure on the worldwide marketing team that includes members from both the North American base and Bern, Switzerland, international headquarters. She is part of the group that wishes as its destiny to take hold of eefer herb production throughout the world. That done and the financial remuneration for the members of the team would be staggering. The stakes were high and, like Sheryl, these people were tough, though with Sheryl her upbringing gave her a softer edge and a better sense of ethics.

❀

By the time the hotel gumshoes got to her room, Sheryl was distraught. She couldn't tell whether Smiley had passed out or had a heart attack and croaked. His pudgy body was still, but she could not bring it within her to check his pulse or for signs of breath. The bedroom reeked of booze, so she guessed he must still be breathing.

The security people arrived and Sheryl pointed them to the bedroom. They gave her that quizzical eye that only security people have really perfected, no matter the hotel. Many of these people are former real police officers, retired. For all they knew, Sheryl was probably having a dalliance with this big fat bastard who they would have to carry off - to his suite across the alcove. Sheryl thought it would be best to say almost nothing, though she did indicate that he must have gotten into her room by mistake, that she was sleeping and certainly would not have let him in. They asked if she knew this upper middle-aged guy, and she told them that she had seen him at O'Fabo's that night and he seemed to be pretty drunk. They left.

The security people knew who Smiley Watkins was, because they had been observing him at the hotel bar before it closed. They opened his suite, across the alcove, and deposited him in the bed where he belonged in the first place. He never woke up or so much as stirred. Curiously, a feather from Sheryl's pillow had broken away and somehow had attached itself above Smiley's upper lip, fastened to his sweat like a mustache and making him look like a garish rubicund street person from Tulose LaTrec's Mont Martre. Perhaps making him look a bit like Salvador Dahli as well.

❊

CHAPTER SEVEN

A Talk With The Boss

GILLY GIGLI WAS ON THE PHONE with Bobbe Birstein. The 64-year-old CEO of E.H. Meris was calling from E.H. Meris headquarters in Bern, Switzerland. He was not at all happy.

Gigli has the look of the U.S. tycoon John Pierpont Morgan. He is plumpish and red-faced and stands more than six feet tall. His pate is thickly populated with blond hair turning a yellow-white. He has a schnozz of ample proportions, owing to roscea, a malady quite coincidentally also suffered generations ago by Morgan. A malady quite coincidentally that could be significantly cured by the 21st century miracle medicines produced from eefer seeds.

"You could be my biggest fool," said the head of the giant pharmaceutical conglomerate. "I send you on missions and you languish. I appoint you to head my special products team and you fail. You have all the earmarks of a second banana and vorse.

"Vee have potentially the biggest deal in our 150-years of business and you move too slowly," he continued. "All I hear about is real estate ventures and the Catholic Church trying to get Ubi back through legal means. Vhat about Meris? My company. Your company. Vhere is our claw in all this? You have been in Ubi for three veeks now and all I get is your woice mail messages and feeble entreaties from you directly from your cell phone that vee are in control and vee vill vin the battle for Ubi. Do I have to go down there myself to strike the deal vith that lightveight, ersatz premier who only knows how to name a country after himself?"

"Gilly, I must continue to tell you that Ubi Ubi cannot be bought," Birstein responded. "He's already made hundreds of millions and he doesn't care about our offers for much, much more. I talk to his top representatives, two assholes if I've ever seen them, and there is no negotiation. They do vhatever he vants them to do.

"I think the lawyers for the Church vill pull off every trick in the book to get the land back through legal measures, vithout paying Ubi a dime," Birstein defended himself. "He will figure his biggest fight is vith them, because vee can't take his land from him. Vee can only buy him out. If he decides to give up the land, he even might try to screw us by selling everything to the Texas real estate interests, leasing back land for eefer production and letting those ya-hoos build high-rise hotels along the shore and having two championship golf courses surrounding them. There'd still be plenty of room for eefer growth. He'd do anything to make it impossible for us to take over the eefer production. He'd do anything to protect his half ass pharmaceutical cabal partners. They've all made a lot of money off the eefer seeds and they vant to continue to do so, Gilly."

"You complete and total ass," retorted Gilly Gigli over the phone. "Do you still not know that vee are the most powerful pharmaceutical concern in the vorld? Vee have remedies far greater than the Premier of a 24-square-mile country and his band of cabal partners, any of vhich could be discredited vithout impunity, you utter puke. Vee can mount our own legal strike. One that will paralyze them. All of these parasites on the pharmaceutical industry, and on our superior company, can be torn to shreds because they have no legal basis for distributing eefer products. I vill take those dicks right to the Vorld Healths Organization. Superior vill vin out. Vee never had to think about these cabalists in the past because, like you, they vere ineffectual and small-thinking. Vhy should vee have? Now it is vh-war. Vh-war, my silly fool. Vill knock thems down like so many little flies.

"I can see I must take this into my own hands," Gilly Gigli reprimanded. From here on you do exactly as I command. The only thing you have to vorry about is keeping your silly-ass cell phone battery charged. And be ready around the clock, Birstein. Do you understand me, you little vh-wart?"

"Vhat are vee to do next?" Gilly.

"First of all Ubi, Ubi, the leader of the cabal, must be neutralized," said Gigli, the ceo. "Like that vonderful song, 'Vatch Vhat Happens,' 'Vatch Vhat Happens!' 'Vatch Vhat Happens!!' you silly little ant of an executive, you flea!"

❋

CHAPTER EIGHT

In Musty Air,
A Power Struggle

WALKING INTO THE GRAND LOBBY of the Ubi Club, one gets the impression that men in skirts and flowing capes will descend the marble staircase. Indeed, there is a Roman authenticity. The Club, once known as the St. William Cloister, and built by the Church in the late 1800s, was home to visiting prelates and bishops - even cardinals - and their well-healed friends for a good part of the past century. It has a fraternal regality that is intimidating to those who are not its members. Great paintings adorn the walls, and white marble sculptures can be found at every turn. Heavy oaken furniture had been the order of the older days of the Club, but Premier Ubi Ubi sought to lighten the imposing feeling with Herman Miller chairs and couches and paintings from his own collections of the modernists. A giant Picasso greets visitors on the wall of the landing of the great staircase. It exudes Picasso's prominent colors and inspires conversation among visitors. Ubi especially enjoys Diego Rivera and it seems everywhere are large and smaller treatments from that artist's cycles of change. Also, there are plentiful works of Alfred H. Maurer on the walls.

Mauer was another painter who displayed radical changes during his career in the 1800s and early 1900s, from impressionistic portraits of women, lusty café scenes and colorful landscapes to dark Paris street people and cubist still lifes.

Many years after the Church abandoned it and the land it sat on, the Club is still the center for power-brokering. Those of wealth wish to be its members and thereby many persons from countries around the world can be noted on its roster, which if asked for, can be perused at the front desk. Only perused. The roster is never copied or allowed off the premises. This is one of the few capitulations to the distant past's policies. For Ubi Ubi, the Club is merely a formality, one that does not particularly appeal to him. He prefers the comforts of his home, the Petite Palais, or when he wants to socialize, O'Fabo's. Largely, he cringes at the power breakfasts and other confabs that are the order at the Club. He does not resent the members or their private intentions, for one must not forget that he is the man who had the Club restored to grandeur, after it had sat abandoned for more than a decade. It is just that in his free country, the Club, to him, represents a confinement. He prefers walking among the 150-foot tall eefer trees than hobnobbing with the denizens of the Club.

Ubi is a social man but he incurs a discomfort when he spends too much time there. In this modern era, Rolex watches, straw hats, Cornelianni slacks, Zegnia shirts, Armani jackets and Gucci loafers and belts are the order. He prefers Turball & Asser ties, Pink shirts and Paul Stuart sport jackets and trousers. And his Raymond Weil parsifal watch. He smokes Te-Amo madura presidentes from Mexico. He does not require Cohibas or Romeo & Juliettas from Cuba. He doesn't resent the fashionable young men he sees smoking these cigars, though he thinks they're somewhat foolish as they blow thick and curling tufts of smoke while slouching their backs in the Herman Miller chairs and talking of their deals.

Thus, it was ironic to Ubi on this day – the day of his meeting with Augustino Crosetti, the lawyer from the Holy See – that he would be having a Byzantine conversation, in the manner of what the original club, the St. William Cloister, must have fostered. Here he is among the yuppies, the baby boomers and the flatly ersatz and he is having a conversation with the strongest legal man from the Church. This is the kind of conversation that should have occurred 60 or 70 years ago, and Premier Ubi is more amused than concerned.

✳

Premier Ubi strode across the broad library of the Club and recognized Father Crosetti sitting in the far corner, with rays of sunlight spotlighting him and piercing Ubi's eyes through the leaded glass above. Ubi thought this lawyer may be a priest but 'he looks like a lawyer to me.' Grim, intransigent with his arms folded on his chest, devoid of warmth and understanding. Boorish.

Ubi had suggested a meeting one-on-one, without the aides of either party. He thought he might gain a bit more power if he could look the prelate in the eyes. He thought it would be the fairest exchange possible, because with Crosetti's usual entourage of a dozen other priest-lawyers, priest-secretaries and rest of his other horde of sycophants pitted against Admiral Schnuck and Artha Crowder, the Ubi camp would be at a decided advantage. Ubi had thought Crosetti would never go for a one-on-one but here he was in a private corner of the mammoth library, which is more of a greeting hall than a place that housed books. Many sofas and chairs, coffee tables and end tables prevail. The sofas and chairs are leftovers from the St. William Cloister. The same kinds of sofas and chairs you would find in any musty old club. Coffee brown, maroon, and forest green are the colors of the leathered upholsteries.

In their private corner of the room, the conversation commenced.

"Premier Ubi it is so good to meet you in person," said Father Crosetti. "So good to meet you. I have seen you on television, on CNN. You are a benevolent man who stands strongly for his constituents."

"I am happy to meet you Father Crosetti," responded Ubi, crossing his arms like an "X" in the manner of Ubian greeting.

Father Crosetti, who seconds before had his arms crossed tautly across his barrel chest, acknowledged Ubian ritual by doing the same. In the Ubian culture the gesture meant, "we are one."

Premier Ubi Ubi is not a religious man in the traditional sense, and although his ancestral origins were drawn to a Balkan rite of Catholicism, he certainly was not a member of the Church. Rather, Ubi Ubi, probably because of his 'round the world travels in his younger days, had developed a sense of spiritual serenity. Not Zen. Not anything very organized, but his own sense of kindness and understanding of his fellow man from whichever discipline of religion or non-religion a person followed. He has close friends who are Catholic, Jews, Moslems, and Hindus. And he had studied Chinese religious writings and has many Chinese friends, a number of whom live in the country of Ubi. He enjoys all these people, whatever their persuasion, and he never has had the intention of wanting any of them to follow just his line of spiritual logic. In fact, he never much thought about what that logic was.

Father Crosetti and Ubi Ubi sat in dark brown leather chairs diagonally across from one another, with a heavy gothic table in between them. The table had a golden-based lamp on it and the lamp was pushed to the back of the table, toward the wall, so that occupants of the chairs could engage each other.

"Premier Ubi, I have heard so many good things about you, that you a broad-minded and cultured man, that you embrace ideas and that you are inherently fair," Father Crosetti started. "I like your assistants but I prefer that you and I deal together. We can get things done more quickly and without the filtration of other minds, and I am speaking of the interpretations of my own aides as well. You must know that my interest in all this concern about what to do about the country of Ubi is not so much a legal one as it is a righteous one. The Church recognizes you and your people, your citizens, as those we respect. Contrary to what some antagonists my say about our intentions, we have the utmost determination to be cognizant of the rights of you and your people."

"Thank you Father Crosetti," said Ubi. "But we have reached an impasse that is difficult to resolve. The Church would like the land back, land that I bought from the Church 24 years ago for $500,000. The Church was only too happy to remove that land from its holdings at the time of purchase. It financed my mortgage of the property and I have paid that mortgage off with a fair percentage of interest to the Church. Now the Church wishes the land back, and I fail to understand why and the 60,000 people who live here with me do not understand either. The cynic's answer would be that the Church wants the land back because of the eefer trees here, because of what they produce, and the money to be made off that production."

"Why would you take the cynic's view, Premier Ubi?" "The Church has plenty of money, plenty of land holdings and plenty of businesses to which it is connected. "We recognize that you, Premier Ubi, have created a beautiful atmosphere, a beautiful country if you will, for people from all over the world to live in peace and quiet

"It is not so much that we wish to take your land from you, Premier Ubi," Father Crosetti continued. "It is that we wish to remedy a wrong that occurred when the property was sold to you at a wholly undervalued amount of money. Our representative at the time, Cardinal Reidy, did not have the authority to sell the property or to sell it for such a little amount of money when it's true value could have been a hundred times greater and today is a hundred thousand times greater."

Ubi Ubi answered, "Well, Father Crosetti, I find it peculiar that now the Church has come up with a value for Ubi that is monetary, that it now sees something in Ubi that it never saw before. The Church held the land for 200 to 300 years, until 1976 when I bought it in a mere real estate transaction for the Church and a large investment for me at the time. At the time I felt Cardinal Reidy thought he had snookered me. I had heard stories emanating from Church representatives who were still living here that Cardinal Reidy would brag that he got double his money on the deal. After all, at the time, the land was desolate, save for the eefer trees and the tent that I lived in. Even this club where we sit today, then called the St. William Cloister, was essentially closed except for a few straggler priests who still lived there and even they wanted out."

"We are only trying to right a wrong," said Father Crosetti. "You bought the land for $500,000 U.S. under an illegal transaction, not recognized by the Church. The land was truly worth at that time at least $50,000,000 and certainly has been that and far more to you in the years that you acquired it. And our calculations indicate that today, with its vast production of what scientists are calling the miracle drug of the 21st century, it could be worth tens of billions of dollars. Pardon the vernacular, Premier Ubi, but we got screwed and screwed good and we intend to rectify the matter."

"As I said, we have reached an impasse," countered Ubi. "The numbers you are throwing around are ridiculous, they're absurd. You can try to take any legal recourse you wish, and my prediction is you will not win. There are many people around the world who will be on our side. You may think you can win legally in the courts but you cannot win in the court of public opinion."

"Premier Ubi, we are not young men, we've been around a long time," said Crosetti. "We can work things out, I'm sure."

"What do you have in mind?" asked Ubi, wondering what Crosetti had up his sleeve.

"We don't need our aides to work this one out," said Crosetti. "I am prepared to work out a plan where the Church would lease you the land. No money would change hands. You would make no lease payments. We are willing to do so for a commission on your annual national product. We would write a lease that would cover 100 years at which time the land would revert back to full Ubian ownership."

"And what might that commission be, Father Crosetti?" asked Ubi Ubi.

"Under the lease, the Church would receive 20 percent of the annual produce," said Crosetti

Ubi Ubi, doing some quick math in his head calculated that this year the national product - mainly the eefer production - would come to about $10 billion, with that return probably doubling the next year and then doubling again the next. For doing nothing but writing a lease, the church would stand do gain billions of dollars a year - and mounting significantly - in the years ahead.

"Not interested," Ubi tersely replied.

"What kind of fool are you? You could end up with nothing, without a country, without the eefer production, if we gain the land back and, believe me, this would not be impossible with the legal remedies we can take. We are willing to give you your dignity, a good deal and the ability of you and your people to stay on the land you call Ubi, and your people will own the land outright in a hundred years. The original transaction that you had for the land with Cardinal Reidy is bogus. Our contentions will hold up in any courtroom, especially a neutral courtroom in some other country."

"Not interested," Ubi replied again

❈

CHAPTER NINE

A Sojourn In Key West

THE VERY NEXT DAY Ubi received a call from the handlers for former U.S. President Hanover Simpson. The Simpson people had said that he would like to meet with Ubi Ubi in California if the Premier could at all come soon. Simpson would be in Bel Air for the next two weeks to review two movie projects he was working on and he would have some time to speak with the Premier during that visit. Simpson would like to chat about the mounting crises that Ubi Ubi was facing in Ubi and he would like to help in any way he could, using his vast connections around the world. Simpson's people said the President had grown a fondness for the Premier during his visit with Ubi Ubi some weeks earlier. He felt he could do more to help Premier Ubi ward off his problems with those people who wanted his land

Ubi pondered this notion only briefly and decided that he would go to Bel Air as quickly as he could. He also decided afterwards he would take the trip to Chile, as his wife Taki had urged him to do. The talk with former President Simpson would bolster his confidence in solving his problems, offer new ideas and perhaps create an action plan to ensure that all would turn out best for the Ubians.

But first Ubi Ubi decided to take a journey to Key West, Florida, along the way. He decided to have a strategy session with his key staff people, Admiral Robert Peter Schnuck, Artha Crowder and Shif-Lee Ubi, his son who is his chief of the interior. Ubi Ubi is flawless in his consideration of other people, a trait that had been passed down through his nomadic family, a family that found it a good idea to try to get along with all people, a trait that helped them immensely in their travels throughout the world over the centuries. One would think that the merger of Mongol, Irish and Lithuanian stock would not set one in good stead so far as temperament is concerned, for these were seemingly vastly different peoples. But curiously it did and there is no better example than Premier Ubi himself, a true man for all seasons. He is naturally a master diplomat. He feels in his heart that all people have common goals and communication and human compassion are central to understanding this premise from all ends of the spectrum.

Besides, Ubi Ubi thought his key men needed some time off. He did not want to be the only one taking time off during crisis. He'd be away in Punta Arenas, Chile, and environs for at least 10 days with Taki, a vacation trip for all intents and purposes. Even his few days in Bel Air with Simpson would be restful, for he would be staying at the incomparable Bel Air Hotel, hidden in the hills of Bel Air just above the Bel Air Country Club, where he certainly would be playing golf with the former President and the President's friends.

Key to this skip to Key West was to get his staffers some rest, while at the same time having a meeting of the minds about what to do about the triumvirate of trouble he was facing from the Church, from E.H. Meris and Smiley Watkins. He noted with amazement that in all his years of living just below China he had never once encountered a problem from the Chinese. They respected his country's sovereignty and while surely envious of the great proceeds from the eefer tree seeds, they made no efforts to oppress the success of Premier Ubi and the Ubians.

So the next day Ubi and his key staff people took off for Key West, not on an official air ship, which he certainly could afford but didn't have, but on American Airlines 7951, a plane that touched down every other day, from its main destination in Beijing. Ubi and his guests did fly first class, however, since this would be a long journey to Miami and then on to the southern-most city in the United States, the Conch Republic, as many liked to refer to it.

Eighteen hours later Ubi and his staffers had taken up residence in a four-bedroom suite on the top floor of the Pier House Resort, overlooking the azure waters of the Gulf of Mexico.

Their first night in Key West, though exhausted from the long plane ride, they dined at Louie's Back Yard, the popular high-end restaurant on the other side of the island and overlooking the Atlantic. They were seated on the first balcony in the open air.

The waitress interrupted their conversations with the specials of the night: seared dry aged beef roulade with sweet peppers, grilled grouper in black olive butter sauce over linguini, African snook stuffed with crab in roasted chili sauce, and the catch of the day, dolphin.

Admiral Schnuck picked the snook. Premier Ubi and the two others laughed heartily, and Admiral Schnuck didn't understand what was so damned funny. He liked snook and couldn't always get it in Ubi.

"You are a decidedly funny man, Admiral Schnuck, without knowing it," Ubi said with a wide grin. "Schnuck has snook," he announced loudly to his compatriots and within earshot of other diners seated on the balcony. Giggles from the others followed. "Schnuck has snook, and what will you have Artha?" asked Ubi again in a deep and loud voice. Artha ordered a pepper steak from the menu, with noodles on the side. Shif-lee went with the grouper and Ubi decided to have snook to make the British Admiral's visage even more twisted and red. "Two snooks we'll have indeed!" exclaimed Ubi laughing loudly. After all the pressure of the previous weeks, he could use a good laugh.

They all clinked glasses of mohitoes, which Ubi thought were about the best to be had in the world right here in Key West. Well maybe they were even better in Cuba, whence the limey, minty drinks originated, he thought.

About 9 a.m. the next day, Ubi and his crew sauntered from the Pier House down Duval Street to the "touron" mecca of Sloppy Joe's. Tourons are what the locals refer to as the brigade of tourists that populate the island from the American north and from cruise ships. But Ubi, knowing the lay of the island, said to his companions that if they catch it just right, Sloppy Joe's is perfect before the throngs inundate it. A few locals will be there, as will Julie the bar maid and the always happy general manager Buddy Duncan, along with the principal owner Sid Snelgrove.

The other three had never seen Key West before and Ubi wanted them to see it from a non-commercial perspective. The place was quiet and clean for a big saloon. The illustration of Hemingway stared down at them from the back of the stage. This was similar to the famous Karsh photo of Pappa in his turtleneck sweater.

Shif-Lee spoke first as they sat down on the south side of the horseshoe bar, ordering beers on tap. "We have a crisis going on back home and here we are having a good time," he said, frowning. "I hope we do take the time to do some thinking and planning while we're here. Things are so unsettled back home we never seem to have the time to get together and plan."

Ubi, looking at Shif-Lee, realized that his son was fraught with the inexperience of youth, that his son perhaps didn't realize that the subconscious mind could perform near miracles if people would let that happen. This holiday would certainly bring some answers to the dilemmas they faced, but if they worked too hard at it, he knew, the answers would never come.

"Let's just have a good time today," urged Ubi, Ubi. "The answers and directions will come as we relax and rest. Let us enjoy the moment and where we are today. We've all been contemplating far too much these past weeks. You know, I wish Jimmy Christian were here with us. He'd lighten things up."

Julie, the bartender, always bubbly, asked the group where in the states they were from. Premier Ubi – with his mix of Irish, Lithuanian and Mongol blood – could easily have passed for an American. He was a mongrel of sorts, a regal mongrel that is, with his kinky full head of grey and white hair and his olive complexion. Shif-Lee looked more American than his dad. Admiral Schnuck, who hadn't spoken yet, not giving away his English brogue, was wearing a tank top and shorts, had his cap on backwards and was two days unshaven and perhaps unshowered. He looked like one of the conchs, a long-time inhabitant of the Conch Republic. Artha, frail-like and tall, looked like he could use some tequila with his beer. And that's what he ordered.

When Julie heard they were from Ubi, she commented that she had seen stories about the country on CNN. Julie and her sweet almost southern accent belie the reality that she had grown up on New York's upper west side. She is hip and has been in Key West for the past 18 years, having arrived at age 20, thinking she'd move on. She is a pretty woman with deep brown eyes and dark brown hair.

Julie introduced the crew to Buddy and Sid, the latter two of whom also recognized Premier Ubi and seemed honored that he might stop by their place. Julie thought of Ubi as a kind of exotic celebrity. Sid bought Ubi and his compatriots another round of drinks and there was much good cheer, as Premier Ubi knew there would be.

The four had another round and then headed up Front Street, then down the boardwalk along the harbor to the Schooner Wharf, where things already were kicking at 11:15 a.m. Michael McCloud, the self-described poor man's Jimmy Buffet, was setting up for a solo stint on the open air bandstand.

The Schooner Wharf is as rowdy and Key West as it gets. Most tourons have never discovered the joint, although some know about it and Michael McCloud, always acerbically witty, ritually made fun of them.

Sitting on a stool between Admiral Schnuck and Ubi was a chocolate Labrador retriever. That's quite common at the Schooner. A couple of stools down was a cocker spaniel, next to Artha Crowder, who was looking dyspetic from the earlier beers and shots of tequila. Ubi looked exuberant. His son, Shif-Lee, stood at the banister behind them, looking out into the harbor, where a group of people had spotted a manatee between two boats right next to the wharf. The manatees are tamer than the nature wardens would wish them to be. They like to eat the small fish and junk food thrown from the pier and they also like to be sprayed with fresh water from a boat hose, which was just what one of the fishing captains was doing as Shif-Lee watched. This is all a legal no-no but the tourons loved watching and sometimes participating.

Michael McCloud's cigarette-induced rough-house voice crackled over the P.A., piercing through the conversations at the bar beneath the thatched roof. The tune he was singing, "She Gotta Butt," was about a woman who used to work at the Schooner. In introducing the song, Michael explained that this was a woman who was "over opinionated and under-informed." She was small-minded, had a small house and small car, but she had a big butt. Michael hadn't liked this woman and one day he just made up a song about her and her big butt. He irritated her so much that she "quit that day, good bye and good riddance."

Sitting next to the Lab, Ubi Ubi thought about his own loyal pet back home. The pet's name is Filigree, not a dog but instead a yellow and black feathered macaw. Ubi figured the macaw knew at least a couple thousand words, as he could speak in many complete sentences. Filigree is feisty by nature and seemingly delights in making fun of visitors to the Petite Palaise, Premier Ubi's home. Some people think that Filigree had been induced by Ubi to be Ubi's alter-ego. Ubi is unfailingly courteous but his bird is the exact opposite. Some think Ubi, with his dry sense of humor, has much fun watching Filigree insult houseguests.

Filigree has a helmet of striking yellow and black-streaked feathers about his head. Very striking indeed. Unfortunately those are all the feathers Filigree has on his body. A skin rash several years ago caused all the body feathers to be lost and never to return. This dismayed Ubi and made Filigree even more cantankerous. Ubi hopes that his friends at one of his partner pharmaceutical companies will be able to come up with a cure using the eefer herbs. So far no progress.

Now Michael McCloud, cap slung low over his forehead and with a cigarette stuck between the strings above the neck of his guitar was into one of his and everyone else's favorite pieces, "Tourist Town Bar."

"...Bimboes and bozos and bikers and boozers, daytime drunks and three-time losers. A roomful of rednecks and fancy-dressed fellas, busloads of blue hairs and dirtbag sailors. It's just another day in this tourist town bar, sittin' here on this stage and just picking this guitar, feeling like a fool 'cause I'm wishin' I was a star, singing other people's songs in this old tourist town bar."

Ubi Ubi could only think that this is what the town of Fung Hi and most of his country would turn into if Smiley Watkins were to get his way and turn Ubi into touristville. Key West was touristville, not Ubi.

"Admiral Schnuck are you having a good time?" asked Ubi Ubi. Admiral Schnuck, now into his seventh Budweiser and fourth tequila, was most assuredly having a good time in Margaritaville as he took glances at the girls in haltertops and bikinis. Admiral Schnuck was feeling no noticeable pain, although even being a naval man, he had trouble looking out toward the Gulf of Mexico behind his bar seat. The boats bobbing on the waves in the harbor made him ill, just as when the old cruiser he commanded was bobbing at anchor. He was fine when things were moving, but at anchor or stationary at barstool, he felt the old sea sickness come on, so he preferred to look at the girls and the bar as he drank.

CHAPTER TEN

The Intrigue And The Lust Mount

ON THE OTHER SIDE OF THE WORLD, Gilly Gigli's private jet had arrived at the Fung Hi airfield. Bobbe Birstein was there to greet him as the portly gentleman descended the Gulfstream.

They went directly to the Ubi Club, where Gilly would be staying, the Marriott not being resplendent enough for such an important figure such as himself. Afterall, he was the ceo of E.H. Meris. As Gilly and Bobbe strode through the cavernous lobby they both found themselves staring at their colleague from the states, Genny Chancellor, sitting on a divan with an older man, a priest.

Seeing the two, Genny leapt from the divan to say hello and introduce them to the man he was seated with.

"Gilly, it is so good to see you," Genny accounted himself. "I hope you had a nice air ride into Ubi. It's been a long time since our sales meeting in Bern. And, please, I want you to meet my friend here, Father Augustino Crosetti. Father Crosetti is a lawyer with the Holy See."

"Good to meet you, Father Crosetti," said the Meris ceo, looking at him quizzically.

"And it is certainly my distinct pleasure to meet you, Mr. Gigli. I have read so much about you and your leadership of your company. You are like a Swiss version of Lee Iacocca. Very innovative, visionary," said the Vatican lawyer.

Gigli, his visage beaming a bright pink, said, "Well, guess vee must look at ourselves as perhaps friendly adversaries so far as Ubi is concerned. Vee both have a price, or should I say vee knows vhat vee vishes to attain."

"You know, Mr. Gigli, just two days ago at this very club I had a session with Premier Ubi and essentially he told me to go pound it, as the Americans would say. I respect Premier Ubi but he is untractable. You shall see for yourself. But he has come against a force far greater than his capabilities to repel."

"My good father, I shall not see for myself because I have no intention of even meeting with Premier Ubi. I am E.H. Meris, $125 billion in annual sales, I do not have to meet vith a tinhorn dictator like Ubi Ubi. I have better things to do vith my time!" Gigli snorted.

"Besides, my right hand men here, Birstein and Chancellor, have been meeting with Ubi's two assistant twits, one of vwhom calls himself chief of staff and the other information officer. They are like talking to vwallpaper. Pure sycophant idiots. They are not as sharp as my sycophant idiots," Gigli said with a loud guffaw as he looked at Chancellor and Birstein.

Father Crosetti, the man of no small ego himself, delighted in the put down, for he feels he is better than the phalanx of priests and aides who work for him. There are notable similarities in Crosetti and Gigli. Like Gigli, he feels that when big work is to be done, it best be done by himself. He can barely tolerate those around him.

❊

Several blocks away at the Ubi Marriott, Sheryl Chan, was the only Meris employee who seemed to be "working" that night. Gigli had taken Birstein and Chancellor out to dinner to further chastise them, and Sheryl was in her junior suite wrapping up a plan to effect the takeover of the Ubian eefer interests. She knew her work would pay off in more ways than one and that she without question could outshine Bobbe Birstein in the eyes of Gigli. She thought of both Bobbe and Genny as two fairly small impediments in her ride up the chain of command at the pharmaceutical company.

Sheryl had mostly gotten over the intrusion and ostensible rape by Smiley Watkins a week ago, though the incident had left her shaken in this far-away stronghold of the eefer tree. And speaking of eefer trees and their wing-like nuts that produced the increasingly world-renowned eefer herbs, Sheryl was going over a list of possible eefer applications that could be added to the already mounting number of ways eefer can be used.

She knows that with E.H. Meris's treasure trove of cash and its incomparable marketing might, the company could take eefer herbs, drugs, cosmetics and other by-products and double its annual sales of $125 billion in the next couple of years. She knows that neither Birstein nor Chancellor, who spend more time kissing Gilly Gigli's ass than thinking out of the box as he wished they would do, don't have the gumption or the vision to go the next step. She also knows that the 12 smaller pharmaceutical companies that Ubi Ubi partners with do not have the financial wherewithal to take the existing products and new applications to another level.

With her scientific background and her good looks and her bubbly nature, Sheryl Chan has a good connection with the research scientists at Meris in America and overseas. She can reach any of the top researchers with a simple phone call or e-mail and get a quick response. So while Birstein and Chancellor busied themselves with the arrival of Gigli in Ubi, for the past week she continued her communication with the scientists who could help her expand the marketing promise for eefer.

One good reason she had such a good connection with all concerned is that she had struck up a more than, ehem, a casual relationship with the assistant director of research, Platsy Schmid, at the Bern headquarters. Platsy is a tallish blond Swissman who is both lothario and genius and some say the fellow who will take over eventually when Gilly Gigli retires. Platsy's boss, Ansel Aignier, is Gigli's age and his best friend and university comrade from many years ago. Gigli depends upon no one but himself, with the exception of Aignier, who laid down some of Meris's best medical, cosmetic and health and wellbeing products over the past quarter of a century. Aignier has trained Platsy in his image, but Platsy is even stronger in ability than his mentor and Gigli and Aignier remain convinced he is the man of the future. Platsy Schmid is credited with developing breakthrough products in both human and animal husbandry science over the last few years that have made Meris big money.

Sheryl caught wind of this early on during her second trip to Bern. She had met Platsy on the first trip and thought him quite handsome but too smug for her tastes. But on the second trip for the company's annual sales meeting she found herself sitting next to him at a lavish white tie dinner Gigli had thrown at his moutain chalet - make that stone palace - 70 miles northeast of Bern in the little town of Vilderbotten, which Gigli created and controls. (Gigliestein is the name of his huge chalet and next to it are strung, on either side, 12 A-frames for guests.) Sheryl was assigned an A-frame with two other female executives, a place she spent precious little time at during the meeting.

With his guile, his wit, his handsomeness and impeccable suiting, shirt and tie and his imperial smugness, Platsy Schmid swept Sheryl off her chair, into the sharp winter wind, down the snow-laden cobblestone path and into his own large and private A-frame. When the meeting wasn't in session they spent much of their time together in front of his fireplace, drinking different brands of Armagnac - J. Gauavin, Larressingle, Chateau du Busca, San Gil, all provided from Gilly's private stock. For a nightcap, after feverish sex, they would switch to the very wonderful Delamain, a delicious cognac and return to the fire. Strangely, they never spoke of the sales meeting or of any business for that matter. They had quickly launched into their own river of lust, which made the boring sales meeting more tolerable.

It was now 11 p.m. at the Ubi Club. Father Augustino Crosetti occupied the largest of suites there, with the ornate furniture intact from the original St. Thomas Cloister – the old lodge for cardinals, bishops and priests and an occasional nun – that is now the Ubi Club. He too had a fire going and was sitting on his sumptuous gothic couch, looking at the crackling flames. He did not look like a priest now, for he was wearing a flowery black and orange kimono and nothing else. Cradled in his arms was the head of Genny Chancellor, who also had on a gaily-colored kimono and nothing else.

CHAPTER ELEVEN

Artha And Shif-Lee Come Up With A Plan

BY NOW THE BOYS FROM UBI had moved down the wooden boardwalk on the Key West harbor to Turtle Kraals and then the Half Shell Raw Bar. The sun at the Schooner Wharf was starting to get to them and they had heard much of Michael McCloud's original repertoire, or least all the stuff he had on two CDs. Good, fun stuff. Shif-Lee bought the two, "Ain't Life Grand," and "Gretastits," the latter of which was named after one of McCloud's wives.

Turtle Kraals is sort of connected to the Half Shell. It serves pretty good food and has a cozy bar, but, after a round of beers there, Premier Ubi led them to the Half Shell, another great bar and a restaurant serving wonderful clams, oysters and shrimp. As usual, they preferred to sit at the bar, scanning the chalk-on- blackboard menus that populated the place, for their orders.

Admiral Schnuck, at age 54, was sinking into a fine stupor. Ubi, who had switched off from margaritas to beer and back, was rested and relaxed. Shif-Lee, at 25 years of age, was moving well with the breeze, taking in the Key West salty air and sun. Artha Crowder, the fair-skinned information minister, who was 47, had switched to quinine water and lime, and seemed to be more animated than usual.

After they ordered, and with Admiral Schnuck sitting bolt upright but sound asleep, Artha Crowder announced that he had divined a method to ward off the oppressors from the Chuch, from Meris and from the gaggle of real estate interests represented by the Texan, Smiley Watkins.

All but Admiral Schnuck listened attentively.

"Ubi, I appreciate your faith in my ability to herald public opinion in our favor, public opinion from around the world," said Crowder. "But I am convinced we must have something to hang our hats on. We just can't curry favor without a cause. We need to draw people to us and make them understand what we are up against from our enemies. The one way to do this, in my mind, is to have a revolt that will gain international attention."

"But, Artha, you know that our land stands for tranquility and peace; we can't seriously endeavor to create unrest, wouldn't that be hypocritical?" asked Ubi Ubi.

"No. It would simply call attention to our plight. I have discussed this at length with Jimmy Christian and he is willing to spearhead this action among all the 60,000 residents of Ubi. No one is more inclined to strike down our enemies than Jimmy Christian. People like him and believe in him, and furthermore, this takes the yoke off of you, Ubi. If you yourself fostered the revolt against the three despots we face and made our people take on such civil action, you might be called hypocritical. That would hurt us more than help us," Crowder concluded.

"There is truth to what you say, Artha, and I know we must act soon to save our country and its dignity in the face of all the money that these foes of ours are throwing at us to make us demure against each of their special interests," said Ubi. "We must act in the best interests of our people."

"Premier, we shall engage in the process as soon as the Admiral, Shif-Lee and I are back in the country. I will call Jimmy Christian today and get him ready for our counter-strike. When you are visiting with President Simpson in Bel Air, you can tell him in confidence about our plan. Perhaps he can help us."

"I will talk to him, though I'm not certain how far we can trust him," Ubi responded. "I think if I can convince him that there is something strong in this for him, for his position as a former leader of the U.S., he might go along, maybe even try to take credit for our people revolting against the evil forces that would repel them out of the country they know and love. His ending as President was not what he would have liked; he had wished to leave office with a bigger statement upon which he could be remembered. This is a chance for him to have history kiss him with more fervor and credibility and accomplishment."

That evening in Key West, Premier Ubi took his men to the Green Parrot for drinks and some popcorn and Tabasco sauce, which was a delicacy there. It is the oldest bar in the Keys and a favorite of locals. The four were on their way to Café des Artistes for dinner of the duck special, but first Ubi Ubi wanted to reconsider what they had agreed to earlier in the day.

The tropical breeze blew through the wide open shutters of the Parrot as Barry Cuda, the local musical legend banged away on his portable piano, which he moved up and down the street on a dolly to whichever bar he was playing that day or night.

By now Shif-Lee, Ubi's son and interior minister, was adamant in favor of the plan for the Ubian revolt that Artha Crowder had hatched. So was Admiral Schnuck, who had taken another long nap in the afternoon and seemed to be particularly alert at this moment.

"Ubi, we don't have military vehicles, boats, guns or anything else, but our revolt will be one of the civilians trying to protect their country," he averred, with the confidence of the naval man that he used to be. "We'll bring international attention to ourselves, to the cause of our people."

"Right," said Shif-Lee, "You head out to Bel Air to meet with President Simpson, father, and we'll go back to Ubi tomorrow to get this thing going. You give us the word, and we'll start while you're still out of the country, so no one can blame you for instigating this. We might start the revolt when you're on your way to Chile from Bel Air. We'll let Jimmy Christian get this festering in the most natural way possible. Maybe by the time you're back in Ubi after a few weeks, everything will be back to normal and we won't be dealing with Meris, Smiley Watkins and that asshole Father Crosetti. Father, I am convinced that with the TV and newspaper coverage we will receive with this revolt, most of the people in the world will be sensitive to our plight and urge that the United Nations take hold of the matter and throw our opposition out of the country once and for good."

"All right, I am convinced," said Ubi Ubi. "Let's go ahead with the plan. Let's run these scoundrels out of Ubi. Meanwhile let us enjoy our several days in Key West."

With that, the quartet left the green bar on the corner of Southard and Whitehead streets, where a young Jimmy Buffet tried out his early songs, and wended their way eastward to Truman and Simonton and the delicacy of some fine, fine duck and several bottles of Clos L'Eglise pomerol at Café des Artistes.

✸

CHAPTER TWELVE

Tall Hats, Golf Course Architects

A CREAM-COLORED STRETCH LIMO arrived at the Ubi Marriott at 3:15 p.m. Getting out of the vehicle were four guys with tall Texan hats, two of them white and two of them black. At the end of the little processional came Smiley Watkins, wearing no hat this day but a big shit-eating smile.

Smiley had sent for the entourage to help him determine just how he wanted to carve up Ubi, where to put the condos, where to intersperse the hotels and where to build the championship golf courses.

Their first stop was the white-pinkish beaches of the Ubi shoreline, today unblemished with so much as bird dung, as Premier Ubi Ubi had always insisted the beaches be kept clean. Ubian sunbathers dotted the beach here and there, some topless, some totally naked. Dogs frolicked, while maintenance crews kept after them. The shore along the Yellow Sea in this part of the geography meshed naturally with the densely blue and white-capped waves. Indeed, Smiley was right. Ubi could be made to look like an Eastern version of Cancun, combining the beautiful scenery with the terra-cotta condominiums and grand Grecian-style hotels that he had planned on this land just below China. With this master plan would also come casinos and the golf courses.

"This he-are is our paradise," said Smiley, waving his hammy left hand and 32-inch arm across the seascape. Smiley had taken to wearing white poplin suits in the moist Ubian air. This day he chose not to wear his cowboy hat because he wanted all on-lookers to know he was the leader of the small brigade walking up and down the beach.

His compatriots included the former PGA tour player, Cabby Thomas, a fellow who is familiar to golf fans for his winning 10 tournaments in the 1970s and 1980s. He is now a prominent golf course architect, having designed courses in Arizona, Florida, Spain, Germany and Malasia.

Along with Cabby was the real architect, his assistant Skeets Remington. And joining them were two of Smiley's men from Kilgore, Texas, Jay Weatherspoon and Harry Gerthperker. Weatherspoon is Smiley's executive vice president, Gerthperker his head of finance.

Like most pro golfers, Cabby Thomas is lean and short, about five-eight. At 51 he could be playing on the Senior Tour but his architectural business has enjoyed immense growth and he can't afford to spend much time away from it. His deal with Smiley Watkins is $2 million a course, along with a 10 percent ownership in them. He perceives what the courses should look like and Skeets Remington does the actual design. They think they can cut three championship courses out of the 24 square miles they have to work with in Ubi. Two will be along the sea and the other back a ways cut out of the eefer forest in the Ubian hills. Cabby will probably spend all of six days in Ubi to determine the lay of the land and with notebook and pencil plot out each hole. He'll then move on to his next assignment in Argentina.

Smiley is deferential to Cabby Thomas because the squat little lout from Kilgore knows that with the Cabby Thomas name on his three golf courses, people of means from all over the world will be drawn to them. Plus, being the celebrity-admiring blowhard that he is, he'll have big stories to tell at the Kilgore Country Club. Smiley claims a handicap of 26 but he really is a 40-plus. Most people don't enjoy playing with him.

On this day, Jay Weatherspoon was pushing for a fourth golf course, but Smiley wasn't sure. He was thinking that cutting too much into the eefer forest could be a bad mistake, thinking that he could probably work a deal with E.H. Meris to sell the eefer seeds to them on an exclusive basis. He knew the demand for eefer would continue to grow and that there was a fine balance between turning Ubi into a seaside golf resort and cutting out the opportunity for eefer profits.

Harry Gersperker, the financial officer and accountant, had no opinion at all because his adroitness is manifested only in being able to look back and determine what went right or wrong with the Watkins Company's investments. He refused to commit to looking forward. Smiley regarded him as a necessary evil. "With accountants ya can stop all progress dead," he often said.

Cabby didn't treat Watkins with much respect, because he knew there was another rich "john" around the next corner that could afford to pay him even more money. He looked at Smiley as a redneck dick who had no class, only bluster. In fact, Cabby was somewhat indifferent to the whole project, not caring if it happened or not. He knew the worst he would get is the minimum 250 grand he receives to visit a project site and meet with the developers. Cabby has the air of too many pro golfers who are most notable for their egocentric focus, a focus that undeniably allows them to be good at this game. He didn't even want to go to the "backwoods" as he called it to look at the site for the third course, letting Skeets do that later in the day with Smiley and his two executives.

"Smiley, this beach sand here is too fine for the golf bunkers," said Cabby. "We'll have to import some golf course sand from the Carolinas if you want these courses to be first rate. A guy flies a sand wedge through this and he'll miss the ball completely, like swinging through cotton candy. You ready to spend the money to bring in the sand?" he asked.

"Shor nuff I am," said Smiley. "This he-are is a $3 billion project when we get done with it. I don't care if I spend a few million on sand. CitiGroup, our number one bank, won't care either. We're going to make this whole joint first rate.

Cabby looked at him with disdain. He just wanted to get his few days' work done and get out of Ubi. He couldn't care less about the other aspects of Smiley Watkins' project.

As they headed off the beach Cabby noticed an attractive woman sunning herself in the altogether. The woman was Lachitcha Lasos, known to many as the "Brazilian Bombshell" for her porn work. At first Cabby was stunned. He noticed the face and the body and they looked familiar. Then, he realized who she was. He had seen her movies, not all of them of course, because at age 39 the raven-haired, big bosomed beauty had made over a thousand films. She, like Marilyn Chambers, was a legend who superseded all the hundreds of faces and bodies that come in and out of the porn movie business on a bi-annual basis. She had made a few million bucks in her time, while the lesser lights were lucky to make a couple of thousand per film, even today.

She clearly distracted Cabby as he and the others wandered off to the nearby foothills to check out the golf course sites.

❋

CHAPTER THIRTEEN

The Admiral And Artha
Return To Ubi

ADMIRAL SCHNUCK AND Artha Crowder had a fine time in Key West, but they were happy to get back to the homeland and go about their duties and the big plan to revolt against the Ubian oppressors.

The first person the two comrades visited upon their return was Jimmy Christian. They stopped by O'Fabo's after getting off their American Airlines connection from Beijing to Ubi.

"How's the old man?" asked Jimmy after he saw them come through the front door.

"He's rested and happy," said Admiral Schnuck. "He's on his way to Bel Air, California, to see President Simpson. He'll meet Mrs. Ubi there and after the visit with President Simpson, the two of them are headed for Chile for their holiday."

"Artha, you look like somebody beat the crap out of you," said Jimmy. "Must have been a rough trip back from Florida."

"I have an allergy to all the shell fish I ate in Key West," Artha responded. "I've been itching ever since we took off from Miami," he added wearily.

"Well, you have to buckle up, Artha," said Jimmy. "We have a lot of work to do to get this revolt going. I know Ubi Ubi wants no violence, but we're going to have to do what it takes to get these predators out of the country and save it from their oppression."

Admiral Schnuck, quite clear of mind this afternoon, advised Jimmy, Artha and Shif-Lee that the best way of handling the situation was a lock-in. Thus, the Ubians, all 60,000 strong of them, would surround the Ubi Marriott and the Ubi Club, not permitting members of the Holy See legal team, the E.H. Meris Company and Smiley Watkins' real estate crew to exit the two buildings where they were staying.

"We will have them imprisoned in the two buildings, cutting off all ability to communicate to the outside world," said Admiral Schnuck. "We will cut off their food and beverage supplies. They shan't be able to call anyone, fax anyone, e-mail anyone. No eating, no drinking. No talking to the media. We will only let them out when they resign themselves to leaving the country. Then we will escort them out and send them on their way. To make it all very official, we may even have former President Simpson standing by with Premier Ubi waving these evil people goodbye."

"Brilliant," exclaimed Shif-Lee. "Just brilliant, Admiral Schnuck."

"Well, if I do say so myself, this should be a better effort than I experienced in the Falkland Islands in 1982," expressed Admiral Schnuck jollily. "I was sent to save the sheep-grazing capital of South America for the Union Jack and I get upbraided by the Argentineans whose people represent less than three percent of the population. Under all the sheep dung, the friggin' Argentineans thought they'd find oil and gas deposits. We sent them on their way as well, but not before I ran into trouble with the destroyer I was commanding," Admiral Schnuck remembered glumly.

"What could have been so bad, Admiral Schnuck?" asked Jimmy Christian. "The British, with the help of the U.S., won that war."

"Yes, we did," continued Admiral Schnuck. "But the big destroyer I was commanding ran aground and we were peppered by tear gas from the Argentineans. We couldn't see a thing, and trying to get off the sand bar, the worst thing possible could have happened."

"What was that?" asked Jimmy.

"The bow thrusters were going out of control, the great ship lurched, a seaman belowdecks fell backward against the arsenal control panel and inadvertently launched two sea to land missiles, but the way the great ship was situated, they became sea to sea missiles and squarely hit two of our cruisers at midships. All aboard were saved but upon the simple act of bad luck, I was de-commissioned. The people of Ubi are the only people who call me Admiral any longer. So sad. And my son Avery Tooter Schnuck was going to follow in my footsteps, but the British Navy would have none of that after this tragedy in the shoals of the Atlantic off a freaking island where sheep grazed. Avery would have been the sixth generation of naval Schnucks. Instead, he sells Madras quilts in a store just off Carnaby Street. What a loss."

"Admiral Schnuck, you will be redeemed in every way once we rid Ubi of its monsters," said Shif-Lee. "You will be remembered as the military mind whose brilliance saved Ubi for the Ubians." "You will be an historical figure along with my father. I'll see to it that the Ubians erect a statue in your honor right at the center of our sandy beaches, near the port of Fung-Hi."

"My oh my, it is so kind of you to remember me in such a permanent way," said Admiral Schnuck, blubbering.

❇

CHAPTER FOURTEEN

Sudden Death And The Bel Air Country Club

ON THE OTHER SIDE OF the Pacific Ocean, Premier Ubi Ubi found himself playing golf with the former President of the United States, Hanover Simpson.

"Hey, pards, have we got a game going here or what?" asked Simpson. "I'm glad you decided to come to California for some sun and fun. Don't worry about those crazy asses back in Ubi. We'll take care of them right quick."

Ubi Ubi is pretty good at golf, even though his country does not as of yet have a course. When he was much younger living in Lithuania he had been a caddy at a club there and on Mondays when the club was closed he would play. He got to a point where he could have been the Lithuanian country-state champion, but he wished to pursue other interests. Now he only plays when on holiday. In fact, he plans to play some with Taki when they are in Punta Arenas, Chile the next week.

"Pards, that's a great sandy out of the green bunker," asserted Simpson as Ubi went up and down in two on

Number 17. "We're beating the hell out of the S.S. boys aren't we? I like to beat those boys every time we play."

They were playing a team skins game against Simpson's Secret Service designees that day. For 25 clams a skin. Ubi had figured in 12 of the 14 skins thay had won, and now he captured the 15th for a major shellacking of their opponents who were 20 years younger than the 57-year-old Simpson and a lot younger than Ubi Ubi.

After the game, they sat on the veranda, had cocktails and smoked cigars. Ubi Ubi actually likes this former President of the United States. Like Ubi, he is a lot of fun, and you never know what he is going to come up with next. Simpson saw too it that Ubi had one of the best suites at the nearby Bel Air Hotel. Two fire places in a stucco walkup just past the pool where Marilyn Monroe cavorted 50 years ago. Not far from the secluded bungalow where Princess Di and her friend Dodi spent a long weekend.

The former President and the Premier planned to have dinner that night in the formal dining room, known as simply "The Restaurant," which was right next to, appropriately, "The Bar," where they would have cocktails after a late afternoon nap.

As they left the Bel Air Country Club, recreational home to Hollywood's richest and most powerful moguls, the President sort of asked Ubi if he would like any special entertainment that night, after dinner. The President winked a hazel eye at Ubi, and, of course, Ubi knew what he had in mind. Ubi was amused and thought he'd leave the offer alone for now. President Simpson, at six-five, towered over the slight, five-eight Ubi, but Ubi had the larger natural corona of elegance and even power in his quiet, though whimsical, manner. They hopped into the black stretch limo with the Secret Service men, whom Simpson had long ago nicknamed, Huey and Duey. Huey and Duey like this duty, for it is much easier than the White House detail they had had with him his last several years in office. Now they spend much of their day sunning themselves at the pool, and when their replacements come, they often go with the President to the Wilshire Hotel Bar to drink with him and smoke cigars. The three of them enjoy the cocktails and kibitzing served by Kyle, the afternoon and early evening bartender there.

At dinner that evening in The Restaurant, Hanover Simpson asked Ubi Ubi how he could help Ubi Ubi vanquish himself of the demons that were attacking the country of Ubi from all fronts. Simpson, though typically a politician, has the air of aristocracy. In fact he, though tall that he is, has more of a continental look about him. He is baldish with the wings of hair on either side of his head slicked back, giving him the appearance of the designer Oscar De Larenta. No one would ever guess, if they didn't know him, that he was born and reared in Idaho. Later, as an adult, he moved to the Texas oil fields and like the George Bushes, he made millions. Eventually, turning to politics, he was elected mayor of Kilgore, Texas at the ripe young age of 36. He went on to become a Congressman and U.S. Senator and ultimately President.

"Ubi, you talk of a possible revolt of your people, a peaceable revolt as you say," said former President Simpson. "My guess is that all the world will be looking on this as a David and Goliath occasion. Their feelings, I believe, will be much in your favor (Simpson knowing that they would be much in his own favor as well if he stepped into this civil action at the right moment). Certainly the world's media would oblige us with extensive coverage in the same manner they did when I first came to Ubi a couple of months ago. But this would be much bigger."

"Yes, Hanover, you bet," said Ubi. "But we must act quickly and directly before the powers that be who are against us get the upper hand. The power of Meris and the Church go without saying, and, you know, Smiley Watkins would work a deal with either of these groups if he thought his interests would be served as well. My aides and some other key people in Ubi are ready to wage a revolt and a lock-in if you will of the three groups we must get out of the country. The idea is that we would lock them into the Ubi Marriott and the Ubi Club, the places where they are staying, to dissolve their power by cutting off their lines of communication, their food, their beverages and everything else. For example, all Father Crosetti would have left would be his Cuban Cohibas during this siege. I don't imagine he has more than a couple of boxes. We could make life quite miserable for them. We'd even cut off the air conditioning.

"Admiral Robert Peter Schnuck, my chief of staff, is arranging this action even as we speak," Ubi continued. "And all he needs to go ahead is word from me to do so. But I wanted to discuss all of this with you before going forward."

"Ubi, this is a splendid plan, and I will help you in every way as soon as I get through reviewing my movie projects here in Bel Air," said Hanover Simpson. I need about a week. You go on to Punta Arenas and we'll keep in touch. It is best that you not be in Ubi when this unrest begins. We must keep up your image as a man of reason and peace. A little later we may be able to arrange a visit to the United Nations to get the backing of the Security Council and as many other countries as we can. But I agree that we must work fast.

"Now let's go over to The Bar for some after-dinner cordials and I'll tell you about my movie projects," Simpson concluded.

Ubi looked at him incredulously.

Welcome to American politics, Ubi thought. But he was not about to act peeved, for he knew to have Hanover Simpson behind his cause was not for naught. Ubi just wondered how incredibly transparent, shallow and callous could one man be.

At a long concert grand a talented musician played some show tunes quietly. Simpson and Ubi sat near the tall fireplace, smoking cigars and drinking Martell vsop, all on Simpson. People in the lounge craned their necks to look at Simpson and the other man who seemed familiar and in a few weeks, though they did not know at this moment, would be on the front pages of newspapers around the world. Huey and Duey sat at the next table.

If one were a gawker, there was even more to look at. Standing at the bar was Bill Maher, the drolly acerbic host of ABC's "Politically Incorrect," and a female companion. Maher was having a Jack Daniels on the rocks and his companion a white wine. And across the way, on the other side of the piano, were the actor Sean Penn and some friends who were all laughing raucously. There were no autograph seekers, as this was a haven for the famous, a get-a-way in the wilds right above the city of Los Angeles. The non-famous patrons were too cool to bother the famous.

Simpson asked Huey for his briefcase. From the case, he pulled out two heavy script treatments to show Ubi.

"This first one here is about modern day pirates," said Simpson with a bold sweep of his hand over the script. "Not many people know that piracy still exists, off the coasts of Los Angeles and Miami, even way up in Seattle, some even on the Great Lakes and up and down some of the rivers. This is the story I want to tell on HBO. It will be a three-part series, might even turn it into a regular series. It will be fictional but based on the treacherous reality of what goes on. Yeah, they steal everything that can be shipped on vessels. They're even involved with white slavery, importing Koreans and Thais into the U.S. and Canada in those containers for packaged cargo. This has it all, sex, murder, kidnapping, robbery, pilferage, bombings and all sorts of high crimes."

"How do you know about this?" Ubi Ubi asked.

"Easy for me. Don't you remember I used to be President of the United States?" asked Simpson. "I had access to a lot of information from the CIA. A lot of people have no idea what those guys are doing, nor who they are. Believe me, this is a blockbuster. I'd do a documentary if I could. But this fiction will be just as good entertainment. And the pirates, they don't look like pirates, they look just like you and me. They dress in suits and ties and direct all this from land. The people they have driving the ships - some in big yachts really - look like your everyday rich s.o.b. in Bermuda shorts going up and down the intercontinental channel. Nobody would ever guess what they're doing."

"Amazing," said Ubi.

"You betcha."

"When will this air?"

"I've gotten most of the money together and we should start shooting early this fall," said Simpson. "We want to get Dommick Dunne as the Mr. Big in this movie, in his first dramatic role. This guy can act, believe me. We're going after some other older actors, too, like Mickey Rooney and Anthony Quinn. Cybill Shepherd will be the femme fatale. Ernest Borgnine. Rich Little. Tony Orlando. Lynda Carter. We want a young heartthrob or two like Stephenie Spears and Lisa 'Left Eye' Lopez. Maybe a country western guy like George Jones or Garth Brooks. We're casting even as I speak."

"This reminds me of the movie, 'Ship of Fools,'" said Ubi, citing one of his favorite films. "Or 'It's A Mad, Mad, Mad, Mad World,'" another of Ubi's favorites.

"Well, it isn't a comedy. It's high drama on the high seas," responded Simpson.

"And now look here," said Simpson. "This is a script for a movie I'm planning for the big screen. "It's title is 'Quebec City.' It's a romantic murder mystery about a Chinese couple who cannot speak Canadian French but find themselves in indentured service to a British rogue who lives in an old castle in the Quebec countryside. There's some comedy in this one but also a lot of romance like 'Romeo and Juliet.'" I envision the whole movie being shot in black and white to emphasize the dark side of love and life. That's my project for next year. It's the sort of movie that can play around the world. Everybody will identify with it and worry that the poor lovers will find a way into the peaceful life they deserve, raise a family and learn to speak fluent French.

"My," said Ubi, "what a different perspective for you from what you were doing just a couple of years ago. "Then you were the world's number one leader and diplomat and now you are a creative man to the masses."

"Yes," said Simpson, feigning a sheepish humility, "this is another way for me to contribute to the peoples of our beautiful earth. It's another stage of my career, one I quite enjoy."

✻

When Ubi got back to his room that night and opened the door he found the phone ringing. He picked up the receiver and on the other end was Admiral Schnuck. Ubi was told that Artha Crowder had been found dead.

✻

CHAPTER FIFTEEN

What Happened To Artha Crowder?

ARTHA CROWDER WAS FOUND hanging from eefer tree "A." Upside down.

There was special significance to effer tree "A," for it was considered to be, perhaps, the mother of all the eefer trees in the Ubian forest. It was located right next to eefer tree "B." These two trees, both standing taller than 200 feet, were bigger than all the other eefers. Legend has it that these were the two trees that propagated all the other eefers some centuries ago.

Ubi Ubi's grandmother, Mildred Ubi, noticed these two trees a couple of generations ago when she led her family on one of its nomadic jaunts through Mongolia and China and finally to the shores of the Yellow Sea on the parcel of land later to be known as Ubi. She felt something special of them. Something mystical, indeed. One day, she picked up a small collection of the wing-like fruits - really wing-like little nuts-that fell from the two trees and noticed the cooling presence that they possessed in contrast to the hot equatorial sun that shone upon her.

She picked them up and rubbed them on her face and then on her breasts and noticed that her prickly heat disappeared shortly thereafter. Besides their cooling presence, they engendered in her a feeling of calmness, a quiet elixir to the grueling journey that she and her family had endured over the months before. Ubi Ubi at the time was a mere child of five. He saw the look of contentment on his grandmother's face and he, too, picked up the eefer seeds and rubbed them on his chest and arms and his prickly heat disappeared as well. He felt an energy from the coolness, an energy that he would forever remember.

It was considerable that Artha Crowder would be found dead hanging from the limb of eefer tree "A." Everyone who resided in the country of Ubi knew the legend of that tree, the mother of all eefers.

Had Artha Crowder committed suicide from that limb, some 10 feet above the Ubian soil or was he murdered?

The autopsy report from the Ubi medical center indicated that the cause of death was a rupture of his left carotid artery. That he was hanging upside down from the tree limb for perhaps hours gave rise to the notion that he was very much alive at the moment he was shackled to the tree by his ankles. The notion of suicide was present because not far away on the soil below was a stepladder on its side. Perhaps he had tethered his ankles, then pushed over the ladder and hung for some hours until death took him over. Or could it have been a murder that was made to look like a suicide?

Artha Crowder, as we have discussed earlier, was a neurotic man, with some deep-seated and unsettled worries about life. To boot, the tumult that was overtaking the country of Ubi had worked its way into Artha's psyche in a manner that was more than noticeable. Even on holiday in Key West the previous week he had appeared despondent and overtaken by his own demons and those created by others.

In any event Artha must have suffered a horrible, lingering death by hanging in his bat-like way. Someone with a blackened humor might have indicated that - being ever-so melodramatic - Artha would take his own life in a way quite uncommon.

But there certainly was the specter of murder as well. And with the maddening intensity to control Ubi and the eefer forest by the outside interests, this theory was quite plausible.

Back at the Bel Air Hotel, Premier Ubi Ubi was on the phone with his chief of staff, Admiral Schnuck, to determine what had happened to their dear friend and confidante, Artha Crowder, the minister of information.

"We just don't know, sir," said Admiral Schnuck from across the ocean. "Artha was really out of sorts on our plane ride back from Key West. He cursed profusely, refused food and drank prodigiously, for him. The stewards had to calm him down and they gave him a shot of something. We had him removed from the plane on a litter. He was still out cold when we delivered him to the Petite Palais and even, Filigree, whom he adored, couldn't get him to smile as he waked. The very next day the caretakers found him hanging from eefer tree "A." They thought he was not well, but in fact he was dead.

"You know how fastidious Artha was," continued Admiral Schnuck. "Our dear friend had Velcroed his tie to his shirt and the bottom of his seersucker suit jacket to his trousers and his trouser cuffs to his silk stockings so as not to look rumpled. Now I know this would appear to be suicide, a pre-meditated event. But, of course, this could be made to look so. I have no idea who could have killed Artha, but if there is a killer, Jimmy Christian, Caz Caswell and Densmore Asault and I shall find that person and dismiss of him posthaste."

"Please, please," said Ubi Ubi over the transoceanic phone lines, "we must not take law and order into our own hands. "I don't believe Artha, as tormented as he was, would have taken his own life. He was so looking forward to going to the North Sea Jazz Festival next month in Holland. I had told him that I would go too, especially to listen to Oscar Peterson and hear Claudio Roditi play with the Dizzy Gillespie all-star band. That was to be a highlight for Artha and as troubled as he was he wouldn't have missed the occasion. My thought is that he was murdered, murdered very, very cruelly. He would do anything for his country and I'm certain that one of our opponents is to blame. We should find that person and turn him over to the United Nations security force for proper adjudication. But we must not take that person's life into our own hands and destroy him as was destroyed our dear Artha Crowder, perhaps besides you, Admiral Schnuck, the best man I have ever known."

✺

CHAPTER SIXTEEN

Cabby Delights With Lachitcha

WHILE ADMIRAL SCHNUCK PROCEEDED into the investigation of Artha Crowder's suicide/murder, things were getting hot at the Ubi Marriott. Smiley Watkins and Cabby Thomas, the golf pro and architect, and their respective crews had returned to the Marriott from the golf site visits.

But Cabby's mind was on anything but golf at this point. He couldn't get his mind off of Lachitcha Lasos, the Brazilian porn queen, who he discovered luxuriating on the powdery Ubian beach that afternoon. That Smiley Watkins kept distracting Cabby from his distraction did not play well with Cabby. The fact that Cabby Thomas was receiving a $250,000 stipend from Smiley for just showing up in Ubi meant little to Cabby. He looked upon Smiley as a redneck little Philistine dick who had no class and no compelling virtues.

"Come hear-ah, comie hear-ah, Cabby, let's us go have us a drink in the lobby bar," said Smiley, as he dismissed his own associates and made it clear to Skeets Remington, Cabby's associate who does all the real course architectural work, that he was not invited. No, Smiley Watkins wanted to sit with Cabby in the large, modern lobby with the rectangular bar directly at its center. He didn't want any of the others around. Better to preen by himself with Cabby. Most people knew who Cabby was on first sight, first because he was a popular and successful player on the PGA tour for almost two decades and second because he was one of the first golfers to make a lot of side money doing commercials.

No one knew who Smiley Watkins was but Smiley thought being seen in a friendly head-to-head conversation with the famous Cabby would make Smiley appear to be famous, too. He wanted Cabby all to himself, telling the others they'd catch up to them the next day. He had a big night planned with Cabby, and Cabby sensed that.

If you could have entered Cabby Thomas's brain late that afternoon you would have known that he had no intention of spending the evening with Smiley Watkins, watching Watkins power lift a 24-ounce Kobe steak and drink a half dozen martinis. Cabby had his own plans, though he didn't know how those plans were to work out.

Pro golfers are often known for their elitist view of others. They often are cock-sure and certainly filled with an arrogance that is connected with their success in a fiercely competitive game. There are exceptions, of course, but Cabby Thomas was not one of them. He was not happy to be seen in a public space with the likes of Smiley Watkins. And, he was determined to make this cocktail session a short one and then go about his real business, the conquest of Lachitcha Lasos, his favorite porn star.

"Sit down, sit down, Cabby," said Smiley, pointing toward the middle of the bar in the middle of the room, where they would be on display for the scores of hotel inhabitants and the hotel's staff who would be coursing by at this time of day.

"I'm very excited about this project," Smiley said braggingly. He had moments earlier ripped the roll of blueprints from Skeets Remington's hands. These would be good props to make everything look important. Fact is Cabby never looked at blueprints, maybe a few drawings of different holes that Skeets would refine. Blueprints? Blueprints bored the hell out of Cabby.

Cabby was becoming more incensed as the fat paws of Smiley Watkins swept over the drawings, as if he knew what they meant. Cabby wanted a quick Chevas on the rocks, maybe two and get the hell out of there.

Smiley was desperately hoping to become friends with Cabby, but Cabby was having none of it, his body language indicative of his feelings, arms akimbo, his face staring off into space as Smiley ranted on.

"Look, Smiley, we can talk about this some more in the morning," said Cabby. "I've got to get back to the room, make some calls. I'm just going to have dinner there. I'm pretty tired from the trip yesterday. You understand. I'm sure you won't mind.

Smiley didn't understand. He figured he was paying this guy $250,000 just to show up, not have to do much work at all, and after the $250,000, the guy was going to get two million a course plus 10 percent ownership. Of course, all of this would be paid OPM (other people's money), principally by CitiGroup, with the collateral being the future golf courses, hotels, condominiums and homes to be built over the next few years.

"Look, Cabby, I do mind," snorted Smiley. "You and I haven't had much time to talk one-on-one. Those other guys are helpful, my guys and your guy, but we need one-on-one time."

Cabby Watkins, thus, resigned himself to spend an hour with Smiley but that would be it. They chatted some more, Smiley had four drinks to Cabby's two, and Cabby feigned fatigue. The noticeably disappointed Smiley bid Cabby adieu and went about having more drinks by himself, looking over the blueprints, watching to see if anybody was watching him.

✺

Cabby sailed up on the outdoor glass elevator to the 19th floor and sprinted down the corridor to his suite. He called the front desk and simply asked for the room of Lachitcha Lasos. To his utter amazement she was listed under that name. Then again, most people wouldn't know who she is because, apparently, most people don't see as many porno movies as has Cabby, who spent thousands of room nights in hotels as a tour player and now as a golf architect. He had seen some of her finest works.

The phone rang about five times. The sing-song voice of a woman answered. It was time for Cabby to work his magic.

✺

CHAPTER SEVENTEEN

Cabby Frolics With Lachitcha, Genny With Father Crosetti

CABBY DECIDED THAT A good rendezvous with Lachitcha might take place at shore-side during the sunset around eight p.m. He thought he would go for broke, just telling her who he was over the phone. She did know him. From TV. He had said he had spotted her on the beach that day and she told him she noticed him and recognized who he was, although she indicated she never once thought he'd give her a call.

"I would like-a to see you, Sir Cabby," she said over the phone. "I knew you are-a fameeous golfer from Ha-merica. I-see you peeform on TV when I was leetle girl-a in Bra-zeel. You a very hand-zome man. I like to a meet you-a."

"How's about 8 O'Clock by the beach pier?" frothed Cabby, feeling a great surge in his corpuscles.

"Ho-kay, I see you by the beech at 8 p.emma..

Cabby was ecstatic.

✤

And at 8 p.m. sharp he found her by the beach, with the tide rising ever so slowly and the sun setting in a brilliant hue of orange, cloud streaks of white and skies of heavenly blue. There she sat, legs stretched out and crossed at the ankles, wearing see-through pinkish harem pants, covering a Kelly green thong, and on the upper half of her torso a tight canary yellow tube top barely holding her ample bosoms, one upon which was affixed the tattooed Portuguese words, roughly translated into English, "Lucifer, Sate Yourself!" Her brilliantly white teeth were framed by thickish lips colored with a purple paint. The nostrils of her aquiline nose flared like Secretariat's after winning the Triple Crown. Her raven mane resembled Secretariat's as well, offering a bluish cast with the sun setting.

She was ready for Cabby Watson and he for her.

This was not romance but sheer lust of the worst order. There was no conversation at first and not for a long time thereafter into the night, as they consumed their passion beneath the jetty that was the welcoming berth for ships at sea who wished to anchor at Ubi.

Lachitcha had been with many men, hundreds, maybe thousands, in her fertile career in the film business but she felt more than sex with Cabby Watson. She felt a warmth pulsating through her every fiber as never before. He felt the same as they blended into one, the waves coursing over their bodies and through their hair. Lachitcha was close to 40 and she knew her career dangled in the balance with so many new products coming on stream in her industry. She had been the Ruth, Gehrig, Jimmie Foxx of her industry, in her era. She knew it was time to hang it all up and become the married vixen she wished to be, until at least after the wedding ceremony.

Cabby has had two previous marriages and three offspring. He has money, he is still young enough, and he thought it might be time for him to settle down with an astonishingly beautiful woman appended to his arm as he cavorted about the world. Besides, even though they had hardly talked except for on the phone earlier that day, he believed she had enough brains to keep up with him. Also, she seemed to be most athletic, and they could go into their sunset together playing golf with other couples.

❀

On the other side of the jetty, another couple cavorted. Father Crosetti, the Holy See lawyer, and Genny Chancellor, the E. H. Meris marketing executive. Beyond their budding romance, they share a dark secret.

They know who killed Artha Crowder.

The last several days, they had found the jetty by the sea, the Yellow Sea, a special refuge. They both liked the salty water and watching the sun come down, while the moon arose. This night it was full and, perhaps, the tides more turbulent as a result.

"Mon ami, c'est magnifcat," said Augustino Crosetti, as the water swirled around them beneath the jetty. "I have for you a special gift of my amour," he said, as he produced from his trunks a beautiful blue diamond ring, which he placed on Genny Chancellor's left pinky. "We are one."

The porky-bodied Crosetti found a great affection for Genny Chancellor, the tall and distinguished Yalie, 34 years of age. Though so young, he so resembled George Bush, the former U.S. President, complete with cowlick. Crosetti had always had a thing for patrician Americans. As they embraced, Crosetti whispered, after licking Genny's right ear, that they must never divulge what they know about the death of Artha Crowder.

Over the past few days, in their intimate conversations, Genny had made a significant decision.

He would leave E.H. Meris in the fall and enter the seminary of the Holy Cross in Bologna, the same seminary in fact that had produced Father Crosetti. His reason for waiting until the fall, September 30th to be exact, was that he did not want to pass by his E.H. Meris bonus check for the third quarter, a check that would be sizable due to his contribution to the unit of the company that was involved with the developing pharmaceutical products. Genny would make a good priest.

Over on the other side of the jetty, Lachitcha, though so amorous, said to Cabby that she was getting cold from the seawaters. All Cabby could think about was that, hot or cold, Lachitcha was better than the time he double-eagled hole number four at Firestone to go 13 up in the World Series of Golf more than a decade ago. Yes, this was even better than when he holed out from the sand on number eight to take the lead in the P.G.A. at Baldestrol, only to lose the tournament on the back nine.

The two were cold and giddy, giddy from the winesack that Cabby had brought to their rendezvous on the west side of the jetty. Giddy and fulfilled from their lovemaking.

"It is time to repair to our cabin in the sky," said Cabby pointing upward to the top of the Ubi Marriott, just a thousand feet away. Golfer that he was, Cabby thought of the distance as a tee shot and an eight iron away. Lachitcha, smarter than Cabby, thought that this would bring a fitting end to her star-studded career and, at 40, she could settle down and be the prima donna that she always wished to be.

❋

CHAPTER EIGHTEEN

Ubi Heads For Punta Arenas, Filigree Tells Off Father Crosetti

HANOVER SIMPSON'S SECRET SERVICE people drove Premier Ubi Ubi to LAX for his flight to Chile. Ubi was still reeling from the death of his information minister, Artha Crowder, and was concerned about the other events that would be taking place in his country in the days ahead. In his phone conversations with Admiral Schnuck, the Admiral assured Ubi that things were well in hand for the peaceable demonstration of the Ubians and that the trail to find Artha's killer was getting hot. The Admiral told Ubi that everyone close to the case believed it was a murder not a suicide.

The Admiral urged Ubi to have the best time he could in Chile. "Jimmy Christian, Caz Caswell and Densmore Assault have banded together to help me on every detail," he said. "And Shif-Lee is organizing as many of our country people as possible to join in the demonstrations and lock-in. It is best that you be far away during this time.

"When you return, it should all be over, and those rapscallions should all be gone from here for good."

"Admiral Schnuck, I will be in Punta Arenas for less than a fortnight," said Ubi Ubi. "Hanover Simpson says he will be happy to go to Ubi with me after Taki and I leave Chili. We're planning on meeting him in L.A. and then flying with him back to Ubi. I hope by then everything is quelled. Simpson says he is ready and willing to take up our cause on our soil as long, I suppose, as his movie deals don't get in the way," Ubi Ubi said with a wry laugh.

With that, Ubi Ubi hung up the phone in the LanChile lounge at LAX and got ready for the seven-hour flight to Santiago, where he would meet Taki; then, over four more hours, they would go on to Punta Arenas.

Taki was getting ready to meet Ubi in Santiago. She was looking forward to her trip to her homeland. The Ubies had helpers in the Petite Palais, aides mainly, who handled a number of jobs. And these people were well paid. As one of Taki's assistants, Mara, was packing up the last of three shipping crates of clothing and other belongings for the trip to Chile, the doorbell rang at the Petite Palais. Mara went over to answer the door, an arbor-walnut door that for some reason stuck upon opening, and to her witness was a priest wearing a black Cossack hat with a red feather, Father Augustino Crosetti.

"Father, what can I help you with?" asked Mara.

"My dear, I wish to see the Premier's wife, Mrs. Ubi. I know she is soon to travel overseas, and I did want to see her before she goes. I am a friend of Premier Ubi's."

"Dear Father, let me please get Mrs. Ubi for you."

Father Crosetti entered the vestibule and stood there while Mara found Taki Ubi. The lawyer from the Holy See sat down on a red velvet bench in the vestibule. He waited for Mrs. Ubi.

"Hello, hello, you scoundrel. Welcome to the Petite Palais. You red-faced piece of shit. Love is everything. It is wonderful. Hello, hello. Do you need anything, you piece of shit? Welcome, welcome. Hello, hello. Watch out, watch out. Go over the fence, dummy. Hey, hey, hello, hello. Go to hell, correct that, go to hades, you asshole. You dork. Hi, hi, hi, hi. Hello. Hello. Drop your pants, cream-puff. Hello. Watch the wood, watch the wood. Don't spit on the floor. What do you want? Don't be an asshole, red face. Hey, welcome to the Petite Palais. Welcome. Ubi Ubi welcomes you. Hi!" said the macaw, Filigree.

Taki entered the room and brushed off the rantings of the bird with the gold and black helmet of feathers and nothing underneath. The macaw who was now about 15 years old had become rambunctious and totally out of sorts. Taki did not want to encourage the bird who would only rant more.

"Father Crosetti, welcome to the Petite Palais. My husband has spoken of you and he has told me of your interest in our country. Premier Ubi, I can tell you, will not move from this country; he believes it has no consequence of others and that it is simply the land of the Ubians."

"Mrs. Ubi, your husband and his country will lose this battle. The Church owns this land, lawfully, and there is no contest at all. We are happy to work out a resolution that is satisfying to all but we will not be put off indefinitely. We are offering a very satisfying resolve to Premier Ubi, but he only says 'not interested.' Perhaps you can persuade him against his intransigence," Crosetti bellowed.

"Hey, fat boy, what are you goin' do for us?" screeched Filigree. "Fat boy. Get out of the Petite Palais, jerk-off, fat boy. Wait 'till Ubi gets a hold of you. You'll be sorry, you'll be sorry, dick-face. We'll fix you. What a faggot. Get out, get out." These were the assertions of Filigree, the macaw, Ubi Ubi's pet.

"Father Crosetti, forgive Filigree's words. He is disturbed and confused and he misses Ubi Ubi, but let me say Father Crosetti, no one here is interested in talking with you. No one. You have no right here, after we have had the land for 25 years. We've done no wrong and we have been good to the people. You don't have cause to change a long-standing legal agreement for the purchase of the land," said Taki Ubi. "I wish that you would leave our home."

"Dick-face, go kiss my royal butt. Kiss it. Go away, go away. This is the Petite Palais. No piggies wanted here. Go away," chattered Filigree.

Father Crosetti took his Cossack hat with the red feather in it and left.

CHAPTER NINETEEN

The Plots Thicken

JIMMY CHRISTIAN, Admiral Schnuck and Shif-Lee Ubi caucused in the back room of O'Fabo's. It was after closing time, about 2:45 a.m., and they knew that they had much to do in the next 48 hours. Joining them was an American, Dennis Columbus, who had been a government official, an egg salesman and a high school math teacher before becoming a private investigator a half dozen years ago. Dennis has done well in the sleuth business, especially in corporate espionage, and now has a second home in Ubi. He is more than a drinking pal of the gang, but also a devoted confidante who deeply respects what the country of Ubi stands for. It was fortunate for Admiral Schnuck, Jimmy and Shif-Lee that Columbus was in Ubi at the time of the crises they were combating. Normally at this time of year he would have been at his home base in New York City working on corporate criminal cases; little did he think that he would be posed with solving a murder in Ubi and mounting a para-military effort as well.

"We know damned well that Artha Crowder wasn't murdered," said Christian, whose office was as neat as the public areas of O'Fabo's. The ex-ballplayer appreciates the success he has enjoyed with the most popular nightclub and grill in Ubi.

"But how da hell do we prove it?" he asked the other three in a deep basso voice that needed no amplification.

"We can eliminate a lot of people right off the bat," said Columbus. "We probably can eliminate all the Ubians themselves, including ourselves. No one who lives here would want to kill Artha Crowder. It doesn't take a gumshoes like Columbo to figure out it must have been one of the visitors from the Holy See, the Meris company or from Smiley Watkins' group. Someone who wanted to send a message to the rest of us. To stop us from resisting their plans to takeover Ubi. Someone trying to scare the living shit out of us." Dennis Columbus mentioned the TV detective because Columbo, whose name was so similar, was a folk hero to him. Dennis Columbus is a bit taller than Peter Falk, who plays Columbo, but has the same disheveled graying dark brown hair and a somewhat goofy expression, without the prop of the bad raincoat. Instead he prefers to don heavily worn Tommy Bahama shirts and trousers.

"The unfortunate death of Artha has done the exact opposite if you ask me," said Shif-Lee Ubi, the interior minister and Premier Ubi Ubi's son. "If anything, we'll do anything we can to run these wretched intruders out of the country and before we do that we will find out which one or ones did Artha in."

"Shif-Lee, we must not forget, much as I don't want to believe it, that Artha could have committed suicide," said Admiral Schnuck. "People say how could he have hanged himself upside down? A suicide? Well, the ladder fallen below him could have been pushed down after he laced his ankles to eefer tree "A" and thus he simply hanged there for hours until he died of the burst carotid."

"I don't buy that for one minute," barked Jimmy Christian, "not for a minute. Admiral, you know that as much as I do, even better because you worked so closely with Artha and knew him better than any of the rest of us did. You don't buy it for one minute either." Admiral Schnuck wearily nodded his head in agreement. It certainly was what he wanted to believe.

"I've been doing some checking," said Dennis Columbus. "This afternoon I was talking to Coroner Habib and she confirms that his carotid had burst, that he did not have a heart attack, that he wasn't stabbed or shot in any way, that he was not strangled. I asked about anything different or unusual, besides the fact that his tie was Velcroed to his shirt, his jacket bottoms to his trousers and his cuffs to his socks so as not to look rumpled as he hung upside down. Know what she told me then? She said she had discovered a pungent perfumey scent on his clothes and on his body. She thought it was Chanel #5 but couldn't confirm. She said it smelled more like a perfume than a man's cologne. Do you guys know if he wore anything like that?"

"No, not like that," said Admiral Schnuck. "No, Artha liked Old Spice, the original Old Spice. He'd never wear a perfume."

"Oh, yeah," said Jimmy Christian, unfolding his burly arms, "we used to kid him about that. We'd say Old Spice Artha, fresh out of the show-ah. Never met a man who was more fastidious and predictable. A real piece of work."

At that moment Caz Caswell and Felonius Assault joined the group in the back room at O'Fabo's. Before their sets that night they had spent most of the day helping to organize some key Ubians to participate in the planned peaceable revolt and lock-in involving the Ubi Club and Ubi Marriott, either in which the enemies were residing. They also observed the mounting influx of people arriving from the Ubi International Airport.

"I'm tellin' you the enemies are growin' in number," said Cas. "We saw half a dozen more limo loads of people coming from the airport. Saw a big group of those Texans with the big hats, a bunch more of those stiff-assed Meris people, and more men in frocks than you would see at a Christmas mass at St. Peter's Basilica. The hotel says more are due in tomorrow."

"We have to move, man, we have to move," echoed Felonius, grinding his teeth. "We get all those people all locked and turn off the air conditioning and stop the food and booze and knock out their phone lines and computers and they'll wish they never came here."

"Do you think anyone has caught wind of the lock-in," asked Shif-Lee?

"No, I don't think so," said Admiral Schnuck. "But the longer it takes to get this done, the more they'll be wise to it. I say we strike tomorrow, certainly within the next day and a half. Best in the wee hours of the morning. We'll cut off the air conditioning first. Sort of begin smoking them out."

"Yeah, and by the time they wake up all sweaty, they'll be able to look out their windows and see our demonstrators, circling the two buildings by the thousands," said Jimmy Christian.

"By mid-day, we should begin to draw media attention, CNN, ABC, NBC, the New York Times, London Times the whole magilla," said Admiral Schnuck. "I know Artha Crowder, who was the best information minister I have ever known, and my dear, dear friend, please let him rest in eternal piece, would be proud of us. It will be peaceful but terribly impactful in the court of public opinion the world around.

"It shan't take long to whisk out the varmints," Admiral Schnuck continued. I give them two, three days and they'll be gone. Premier Ubi Ubi can come back and clearly claim Ubi for the Ubians and don't be surprised if he brings President Hanover Simpson with him. Somewhere along the way, I hope we shall find the killer of Artha Crowder. That person or persons shall remain here until we can turn them over to the U.N. security force for the appropriate criminal prosecution in a neutral country, unlike ours, that has a court system. The only drawback to having no lawyers or judges of our own and no court system, and no electrical chair for that matter, is that we won't be able to roast these monsters on our land. But let's solve the crime first."

✸

CHAPTER TWENTY

Gilly Tries To Fix Ubi Ubi Real Good

GILLY GIGLY RAN INTO Father Augustino Crosetti in the breakfast dining room of the Ubi Club and only gave the Vatican lawyer a cold-eyed glance. He did not like what he had been hearing about the efforts of Father Crosetti and his brigade of priest/lawyers and priest/secretaries to undermine his own efforts to take over the country of Ubi. The head of E.H. Meris did not say hello or even indicate that he had seen Father Crosetti as there paths crossed in front of the buffet table. If Gilly could have done so without a commotion being witnessed by the many others in the breakfast room, he would have elbowed Father Crosetti to his ribs. To Gilly, as is so true to others, including Admiral Schnuck, Father Crosetti is evil, a man who would play the game only under his rules, rules that are dubious at best.

As Gilly Gigly sat down by himself at a table near the center of the room, he felt at home for a moment. He looked down at the shaved ham, the eggs, mixed fruits, breads and biscuits and felt he was back at Giglistein, his giant chalet in Vilderbotten, Switzerland. Fit for the king that he is, no doubt.

Seated directly behind him, with his back to Gilly was Smiley Watkins, having his own breakfast alone.

Smiley rose to get more food for his Texan stomach and bumped his chair against Gilly, who spilled his coffee on his coat sleeve. Gilly snorted and gave the fat man a stair. Smiley didn't even know what he had done and walked back to the buffet.

When he returned to his table, he noticed Gilly Gigli out of the corner of his squinty right eye. With only the audacity that was his and his alone, he pulled out a chair at Gilly's table, put his plate down and, without saying a word, invited himself to sit with Gilly.

"I know who ya are. I know, yessiree," said Smiley. "Yar tryin' to out-bade me for this he-are land. Am I right or not? What'd ya say?"

"Vere did you come from, you louse?" cracked Gilly. "First you bump into me, making me spill my coffee on my sleeve, then you have the pure boorishness to sit at my table. Who do you think you are?"

"Now calm ya-self down. Calm down," said Smiley. "I just wanted to introduce myself. Name is Smiley Watkins, Kilgore, Texas. I'm a real estate developer.

"I know exactly who you are, exactly, and that is exactly vhy I don't vant you sitting at my table or ever talking to me, you slime," groused Gilly.

"I was just gonna suggest we might be able to work out an alliance or a partnership, together, where we would both win," said Smiley. Ya want the eefers and I want the land on and near the sea. Why can't both ideas work?"

"Look right now, look," retorted Gilly Gigli. "I have no interest in you, no interest vatsoever. Do you hear me? Vhat I and my company do vill never have anything to do vith you. You are a bad example of an American. You are a red-neck scum!"

Smiley, now getting up and not giving up, tried to shake Gilly's hand, and Gilly slapped it away, with a loud clasp, as two beefy hands met for a split second.

"Just remember this Mr. Gigli, Smiley doesn't quit. We can work this out to both of our benefits, and let me say we represent a formidable force against those lawyers from Rome, don't ya think? Here's my room number. Call me when yar ready to talk," said Smiley, slapping down his business card with the suite number 1619 written on it.

"Not on your or my life, jackass."

After breakfast, Gilly hailed Bobbe Birstein to his suite. Bobbe couldn't reach Genny Chancellor, who was supposed to come as well. Genny was consorting with the enemy. These last few days he was spending more time with Father Crosetti than on his duties with the E.H. Meris Co.

"I vant Premier Ubi Ubi arrested," said Gilly Gigli.

"How can vee do that?" asked Birstein.

"He is breaking the law by improperly distributing the eefer seeds to his cronies in those small pharmaceutical companies. He has no right to do so. And he does not have the sanction of the World Health Organization," countered Gilly.

"There is a contact that I have been given at the W.H.O., Clement Athelwhite, who vill help us get a staying order on Premier Ubi so that he vill have to cease and desist until he at least has met the standards on the distribution and manufacture of these herbs and drugs. His collection of upstart drug firms vill never meet the standards. This vill open the doors for us to take over the production and force Ubi Ubi to sell his interest in this land to us. If he doesn't, he just might find himself in jail. Vee are gaining the upper hand, no thanks to you my sycophantic associate," chided Gilly.

"I vant you to call Clement Athelwhite and start the wheels in motion now and not a minute later. Do you understand me, Bobbe Birstein? Are you able to take the ball from here, schtu-bum?" Gilly continued. "I vant you to fix Ubi Ubi and fix him good."

"I vill, I vill," said Birstein, wondering if his boss's imploring edict could be carried out. He knows he is operating on thin ice with the CEO and needs a victory to get himself upgraded on Gilly Gigli's chart. It has been some time since he was one of the golden boys of E.H. Meris. And as bumbling and indecisive as he could be, this is one mission he couldn't afford to blow.

Birstein went back to his junior suite at the Marriott and started working the phone. If there is one thing he wants to do most, it is to break the back of Ubi Ubi and his supporters and wrest away the power they have over the country of Ubi

He is probably smart enough to know that the W.H.O., a part of the United Nations, works with other authorities to ensure the health and wellbeing of the world's citizens. He knows, too, that technically it might be hard to prove that Ubi Ubi and the Ubians are actually doing anything harmful through the processing and distribution of eefer products. But he can't believe these authorities wouldn't succumb to the clout of E.H. Meris. After all, it is the biggest and most powerful pharmaceutical company in the world. Why would the authorities side with a dozen dramatically smaller drug companies when they knew E.H. Meris has the research capabilities, the worldwide processing and distribution capabilities and the money, big money, to ensure that all peoples could avail themselves of the miracle drugs and herbs produced by eefer. Isn't it in the best interests of everyone that Meris be involved as the key producer of these products?

Though he could be a real bungler, Bobbe Birstein knows enough that he can turn his low rating at the company into a crackling win for himself if he can complete the simple mission given to him by Gilly Gigli

That afternoon he amazed himself at how easily it was to get Clement Athelwhite, a New Zealander who worked at W.H.O headquarters in Switzerland, to take action in favor of Meris. Clement Athelwhite would do anything for Meris. He had some very good reasons to do so, reasons that never entered Bobbe Birstein's less than agile mind.

❀

CHAPTER TWENTY-ONE

Ubi Ubi In Chile

ON THE LANCHILE FLIGHT to Punta Arenas via Santiago, Premier Ubi had read an article in the Los Angeles Times that he found amusing. He noted that in Unalaska, Alaska, U.S. Coast Guard and immigration officials had ended a search the day before to find the source of a mysterious pounding sound aboard a ship.

"No signs of any stowaways were found during searches late Wednesday and yesterday of 17 of the 1,556 cargo containers on the 860-foot Manoa," read the Associated Press article.

"Officials were at a loss to explain what the crew had heard. 'I believe the crew heard tapping. I think they were very sincere about that,'" said the captain of the ship.

"The incident renewed concern about stowaways and human smuggling attempts on the West Coast," the article continued. "Human cargo is much more lucrative than drugs right now," said the director of Immigration and Naturalization Service in Alaska.

"Over the past 18 months, 303 people have been taken into custody after being found aboard containers from cargo ships bound for Seattle, Los Angeles, Vancouver, British Columbia, and other ports, INS officials said."

Ubi Ubi thought back to a couple of days earlier when the former President Hanover Simpson told him about his plans for the HBO movie on modern-day piracy. Maybe Simpson was on to something, Ubi thought - life imitating fiction. He wondered who was shipping these people into these ports and for what reason. Perhaps we'll all find out when Producer Hanover Simpson comes out with his first movie, the first project of his new career, Ubi thought.

He also thought to the meeting he'd be having with Takita Salernas del Rios-Ubi – Taki, his wife. With all the chaos back home, it will be nice, he thought, to spend some time with his wife in her homeland, especially to go to Punta Arenas, in the Patagonia region where she was born and reared. She would be meeting him in Santiago from Beijing and they would take a Ladeco jet straight south along the majestic Andes Mountains to the bottom of the civilized earth, just above Antarctica. He had always found the land down there a spiritual experience. Maybe, he thought, he could truly clear his head and come up with the answers needed to solve the economic and political power crises back in Ubi. Maybe it was best to try to think of nothing at all, and the sub-conscious would take over.

He waited only briefly in Santiago for Taki's jet to arrive and soon they were on their way for the four-hour trip to Punta Arenas.

Taki could see that her husband was weary and she knew he could use this rest in this town that once had been so rich but had lost much of its luster with the opening of the Panama Canal in 1914. Prior to that, Punta Arenas was a primary commercial center, with all the ships passing through eastward or westward on their journeys, stopping for food stocks, fuel and a brief recreational break. Cape Horn was a busy pathway back then, but save for the mining and agricultural industries, today it is quiet, though steeped in history and lore. Taki had thought it a nice town in which to grow up, this place of 100,000-plus people, right above the Straits of Magellan.

They settled themselves into the Hotel Jose Nogueira at the Plaza de Armas, a place with a beautiful loggia, good food and an overall lovely atmosphere. This would be their base as they took day tours through the Patagonia area and the National Park. They had dinner that night in the hotel dining room, toasting each other with pisco sours and enjoying Argentinean steak, amid the haunting sounds of a young Chilean guitarist.

The next day they decided to head for the National Park, actually Parque Nacional Torres Del Paine. It is a journey of some several hours by bus on some good roads, some not so good. But the Ubies knew when they got there that the peacefulness of one of the greatest nature reserves in the world would be good for their souls. They could have stayed at the Explora, a newer luxurious hotel on the parkland site, but instead decided to camp out for a couple of days.

It gave them pause to witness the flora and fauna, especially the rheas, the four-foot-high ostrich like birds scampering about, and the grazing guanacos of the llama family. Also, they could witness the Patagonia weasel and grison peering through the long grassy areas.

Torres del Paine is noted for its impressive mountain ranges, surrounded by vast forests, dotted with lakes, glaciers and open country. Flowering plants of almost every imaginable color embrace the valleys. The weather there can change in a minute, but this being the Chilean spring, which in North America and Europe marks the beginning of winter, the Ubies enjoyed their days and nights under the sun and the stars.

The Ubies camped out in the southeastern area of the park above the small city of Puerto Natales. From their bluff above the waters they could see the wide-spanned condors flying overhead and, in the ponds and lakes, black-necked swans, kelp geese, ibis and flamingos. In the trees were austral parrots and Chilean owls.

The rhythms, noises and fresh smells of the park fueled the flames and the passions of the Ubies and they took advantage of all this as they embraced and made love as the orange Chilean sun set down behind the mountaintops. They did the same as it came up in the morning over the tributaries leading into the spot where the Atlantic meets the Pacific. During the day they would sit on large boulders, eating sandwiches prepared by their guides and taking swills of pisco, the Chilean national drink that is like a cross between tequila and grappa and has a nice kick to it.

After two days and nights they took the morning bus run back to Punta Arenas. When they got off the bus there they took a short walk from their hotel to the Plaza Munoz Gamero, which is surrounded by some of the grand manses of the sheep-ranching families of the 19th century. At the center of the plaza is a great bronze statue of Magellan with a mermaid and two Fuegian Indians at his feet. Legend is that if you rub the 10-foot-high Magellan's big toe, a toe that is the size of a large shoe, you will return. Ubi and Taki had done this together five times before and they have returned five times. As they did so for the sixth time, they noticed police officers coming toward them from three sides, some in blue uniforms and some in white.

"Premier Ubi, we must place you under arrest," said a captain in the white uniform of the state police. He and a half dozen of his men, surrounded by another half dozen of the dark blue uniformed members of the Punta Arenas police, closed in on the Ubies and led them to the nearby jail.

❀

CHAPTER TWENTY-TWO

The Revolt

"ABC World News Tonight with Peter Jennings"...

"Good evening ladies and gentlemen... Today in the small country of Ubi, a civil revolt is taking place. It all has to do with the jailing last week of Ubi's premier, Ubi Ubi. Ubians are railing against what they insist is a conspiracy to move Premier Ubi out of office and to take over the country he founded 24 years ago.

"Ubi, the country named after Premier Ubi, has a land mass of just 24 square miles and is located along the southern tip of China on the Yellow Sea. It is home to the unusual tree-like plant called the eefer... and that is what most of the trouble is about. Let's switch to John McWethy standing by in the Ubian center of Fung-Hi. John are you there?"

"Yes, Peter, and as you can see over my shoulder, hundreds of Ubians are marching in protest of not only the jailing of Premier Ubi in Chili but also against what they consider to be co-conspirators in an effort to take over the country of Ubi for their own special interests. Among the strange array of those special interests are the Catholic Church, the E.H. Meris pharmaceutical company and a Texas real estate consortium, led by Tommy "Smiley" Watkins.

"Peter, as we can discern at this early moment in the revolt, it appears the Catholic Church would like the Ubian country returned to its ownership, after having sold this remote land mass to Ubi Ubi for $500,000 nearly a quarter century ago. And we understand, the E.H. Meris company would like to take control of the eefer tree herb production, as the eefer herb is known to cure everything from yeast infections to shingles and anxiety to alcoholism. And most recently, eefer has been found to control Attention Deficit Disorder, without the usual side effects of other medicines. A dozen or so smaller pharmaceutical companies, under licensing from Premier Ubi, now process the herb. As for 'Smiley Watkins,' he and a group of partners from Kilgore, Texas, have made it clear that they would like to turn Ubi into an upscale resort, tearing down most of the eefer trees and building a little riviera along the Ubian coast line. Back to you, Peter."

"Thank you, John. Now let's switch to Carlo Salas, reporting from Punta Arenas, Chile, where Premier Ubi has been jailed for the last six days. Carlos, can you tell us what this legal skirmish involving Ubi Ubi is all about?"

"Peter, it all started when Premier Ubi and his wife, Taki, decided to vacation in her native city, the old Chilean commerce town of Punta Arenas, which is located just above Cape Horn, near Patagonia, truly at the bottom of the earth. One day last week, they were looking at the statue of Magellen, in the heart of Punta Arenas, just like any other tourists, when Chilean national police arrested them. Ubi is being charged with selling pharmaceuticals without proper permits to companies on four continents. Seemingly, the legal pressure is coming from the giant E.H. Meris Company that is seeking to process the eefer seeds but has not been offered a license by Premier Ubi. But, Peter, that may be the tip of the iceberg, because there are Ubian loyalists even here in Chile who insist there are other interests at hand in wishing that Premier Ubi be ousted from his country."

"Carlos, what do you think is going to happen in the present time for Premier Ubi?" asked Peter Jennings.

"As we speak, the World Rights Foundation has sent representatives to talk with Chilean officials about Ubi Ubi's immediate release. We don't know where all this will lead, Peter, but later this week we should have an answer. Carlo Salas reporting from Punta Arenas, Chile."

What a contrast from the earlier peaceful moments after they first arrived in Punta Arenas. Ubi and Taki Ubi had just traveled some 100 miles northeast into the Patagonia region, near the Chilean National Forest. It was just a day before that they feasted on roast pig, as wild horses and pygmy ostriches and osprey ran through the land at will. From a bluff, the Ubies found themselves stunned by the scene of the great Atlantic and Pacific oceans meeting, blending as one. Ubi had expected more of a rumbling where the two oceans met. He was amazed at the tranquility of the scene, a scene not unlike the feeling he had in his home country, one of beautiful serenity.

Today, they find themselves incarcerated in Punta Arenas. Mrs. Ubi was not technically arrested but she chose to be jailed with her husband. They shared an 8x10 cell, what a far cry from where they were just 24 hours ago.

At first the arresting captain, Lamos Estacias, would not indicate the reason for the arrest. "I am waiting for papers, but you, Premier Ubi, have apparently broken international law and it is my job to take you under custody," he said in fluent English. "I am more than happy to release Mrs. Ubi, as on her passport it indicates she is a Chilean citizen and we have no reason to detain her for any criminal purpose. Heh, heh, and I am about the same age and remember her as Miss Chile and runner-up in the Miss Universe Contest, which I saw here in Punta on black and white TV in 1964. You are a heroine to me and many others, Mrs. Ubi."

Ubi urged Taki to go back to the Hotel Jose Nogueira, but she refused to leave him in the jail by himself. In his 72 years, this was the first time Ubi Ubi had seen the inside of a jail cell. He was stoic but Takita was not. She wanted to call Admiral Robert Peter Schnuck, their chief of staff, in Ubi, but Captain Estacias would not let them because he had not received papers yet, only the order from the state police's high command that he arrest Premier Ubi.

"Why don't you go back to the hotel, Taki?" implored Ubi. "There you can easily call Admiral Schnuck and have him see about getting me released."

For the first six hours, Taki refused any thought of this, but later in the afternoon, she complied, figuring they had no lines of communication in the Punta Arenas jail. She was angry and scared and she feared for what Ubi Ubi would have to undergo in the days ahead. He was the last man on earth who deserved to be locked up, she thought, and she let Captain Lamas Estacias know this in no uncertain words.

"How can you put a man in jail when there are no formal charges on him?" she asked in Spanish. "What kind of swine are you?" she asked, though knowing Lamas Estacias was hardly more than a messenger boy to this state action.

"I am sorry," answered the captain in Spanish. "I am sorry."

"Why do you need a dozen police officers to arrest my husband?" challenged Taki. "He has no guns, no knives, no hand grenades in his pockets. He has never been arrested for anything until now. He is a man of peace and human elevation. When will we know what is going on and why?" she questioned.

"Madame Taki, I am only following orders," said Captain Estacias. "It is best you go back to your hotel now and talk to your legal people; perhaps in a few hours more we will have the paper work and we may be able to release your husband."

When Taki got back to the hotel, she looked up what embassies might be in Punta Arenas. Ubi, being such a small country, had no embassies of its own but would rely on those of other countries that were friendly to it. She noted that Belgium had an embassy in Punta and she put in a call to the ambassadore, whose name is Yrral Lieber. He indicated an interest in helping, as he knew who Premier Ubi is. He had the sense that Ubi Ubi was falsely arrested. He would start work on this but he urged Taki to get in contact with her people back in Ubi. The first call she placed, of course, was to Admiral Schnuck, who at this very moment was up to his arse in alligators.

❊

CHAPTER TWENTY-THREE

Back In Ubi, A Media Circus Is Under Way

"**MRS UBI, WE'VE GOT THE** oppressors locked into the Ubi Club and the Ubi Marriott and our peaceful demonstrators, our country men and women, are encircling both buildings by the thousands. Media people are pouring in here from all over the world," said Admiral Schnuck, clearly out of breath from the sleepless last few days.

"Things are moving forward here and we'll make our points to the world, but right now the biggest concern is for the safety and wellbeing of our Premier," he continued over the long distance line. "It seems the reason he is being incarcerated is that Gilly Gigli pulled off some sort of stunt with the World Health Organization, saying that Ubi Ubi has broken the laws through the distribution of eefer seeds through our 12 pharmaceutical partners, even though we have been doing so for years."

"Admiral, the people here in my home country will not explain anything," said Taki. "They're still awaiting the paperwork before they can take any action about releasing

Ubi. The ambassador from Belgium is trying to help us but we are in a quandary about what to do."

"Don't worry, Mrs. Ubi, we will find a way to get him out of jail soon, I hope," said Admiral Schnuck.

"I wish we were back in our country," said Taki. "We should be there helping the cause."

"No, no, Mrs. Ubi, you shan't be here now. We don't know the ramifications of the revolt and lock-in. I don't think there will be violence, but we can't tell for sure. Besides, we have good reason to believe Artha Crowder was murdered. It was made to look like a suicide, but we know better. You and the Premier could be in jeopardy were you here," the Admiral said over the line. "Our best guess is that one or more of the foreigners committed this crime. Jimmy Christian and the private "I" Dennis Columbus are pursuing the criminals. Meanwhile, Shif-Lee is coordinating all aspects of the revolt. Your son is doing a good job for a man so young."

"I'll be staying in our suite at the Hotel Jose Nogueira until we get the Premier out of jail. Then, I don't know what we shall do," said Taki, the dark waves of her hair curling from the moist Chilean climate but still looking stunningly beautiful in spite of her distress. "The former President of the United States, Hanover Simpson, had talked to Ubi about going to the United Nations and together making a plea for the wellbeing of our country and its people. Maybe we should go directly to New York from Chile. But the big question is when Ubi Ubi will be released. If the worst of events happens he might be tried in some neutral court. That is an issue that is unfathomable to me."

"Please, Mrs. Ubi, understand that we'll do everything we can from our end to get Premier Ubi released. This is false imprisonment if there ever was one," the Admiral said. "Anyone with any ounce of mercy would see this for what it is - a goliath pharmaceutical company trying to brush aside Ubi and his smaller business partners. Gilly Gigli thinks he can always get what he wants but he shall not take over our country for his own egocentric and evil economic interests. We will prove to the world that we are being ridden over roughshod by the pharma people, the crazy Vatican lawyers and that rotten fatso from Texas. You know, I hate to say this, but in a way I am happy that Artha is dead and does not have to witness what we are going through. It sure would kill him if he did."

Soon after Taki got off the phone with Admiral Schnuck, a call came in from the Belgian Ambassador in Punta Arenas, Yrral Lieber. He felt sorry for the plight of the Ubies and wanted to move quickly to resolve the situation.

"I have been in contact with the World Rights Foundation; they are sending people here to push the state police to release the Premier and that might be possible by tomorrow," said the Ambassador. "I will personally visit Ubi Ubi this afternoon and see that he is all right. But I don't think you should go back to the jail... they might consider that you're in conspiracy with a suspected criminal and jail you too. And my other point would be that they look at you as an ex-patriate, a former Miss Chile and runner-up in the Miss Universe competition who turned her back on her homeland. I hope I am wrong in that last supposition."

"Ambassadore..."

"No, no, please don't call me Ambassador, call me Yrral, I'm your friend and I want to help you."

"Well, then, Yrral, why are you so willing to take this on?" asked Taki. "It might not be in your best interests to be associated with this problem. And it might not be good for Belgium."

"Poof, poof," said the Ambassador. "I am doing what is right because this is the only moral thing I can do." The Ambassador is a charming man, well clothed and with a dark ring of hair around his bald head. He is as distinguished as a career diplomat and trade merchant should be. "First, I am going to visit the Chief of Police in Punta, then I shall go over to the jail and converse with Ubi Ubi.

"I will then come visit you at the hotel to bring you up to date on how things are going. The folks from the World Rights Foundation will join me tomorrow for more talks with the Chief of Police if that is necessary. By the way, I don't know if you are aware, but the international media are having a field day with this situation. CNN and all the other big networks are reporting live from Ubi and some have sent representatives into Punta Arenas. I saw a man from ABC reporting live from in front of the Magellan statue where Ubi Ubi was arrested. He was talking to Peter Jennings. To my mind, all of this activity is a plus for Ubi Ubi's cause. The media will try to get a hold of you I am sure, but I think it best for you not to go before the cameras until we understand more about what is going on here. For now, let me take the media inquiries. I am making arrangements with your hotel to have your phone line privatized so you don't have to sit there with the phone ringing constantly."

"Yyral, I can't thank you enough for what you are doing," said Taki. "When this is all over I should like to invite you and Mrs. Lieber to visit with Premier Ubi and me at our home, the Petite Palais."

"Thank you, Taki. Mrs. Lieber is deceased, so I will have to go it alone, I'm afraid. Perhaps my assistant, Bretta Schiffna, a Croatian, would like to go. Boy, is she a looker. But for now I've got much work cut out for me," said the Ambassador, as he hung up the phone.

Taki is a strong woman, very strong. But at this moment she could not hold back the tears any longer. She was deeply concerned for her man.

❁

CHAPTER TWENTY-FOUR

And Now The U.N.
Gets Involved

CARVER METTLE IS A BUSY MAN these days. The United Nations public affairs attaché has been monitoring the Ubian revolt closely since it erupted two days ago. He is not certain whether Premier Ubi Ubi is guilty as charged but he is looking at the various angles of the Premier's jailing yesterday.

And he has been in close touch with the World Rights Foundation, whose concern it is that Ubi Ubi was wrongfully arrested.

"Apparently, there is a fellow in the World Health Organization in Geneva, which as you know is derivative of the United Nations, and he somehow got this order going to get Premier Ubi incarcerated and perhaps tried on breaking world law," Mettle told Admiral Schnuck by phone. "The man's name is Clement Athelwhite. I've been trying to reach him but to no avail. Have you heard of him?"

"No, no, can't say I do," said Admiral Schnuck, who on top of all the mess he is trying to handle has been suffering from a virus that causes him to sneeze excessively. And it gets worse when he drinks. The guy just can't catch a break. "Achoo . . . Achoo . . . I . . . Achoo, Achoo, Achoo, Achoo . . . I . . . Achoo . . . I'm having a little trouble talking today because of . . . Achoo . . . some . . . Achoo . . . damned virus I picked up."

"I'm sorry, Admiral Schnuck," Carver Mettle responded. "Do you drink scotch by any chance?"

"Yes I do, but lately it even seems to make the virus worse."

"Well, let me give you a tip. Have you tried Bunnahabhain?" Mettle asked.

"No, that's one of the few I haven't tried."

"Bunnahabhain comes from the Isle of Islay, just off the west coast of Scotland. It's soft and mellow and has just the hint of peat in it. It's good for the stomach, the throat and the soul. It will help you, trust me," said Mettle.

This mere suggestion made Admiral Schnuck feel immediately better and he called Jimmy Christian on his other line to see if they had any Bunnahabhain at O'Fabo's. He was so happy when he found out that they did and that Jimmy would drop some off at the Petite Palais in the next half hour. For a man who likes to drink as much as Admiral Schnuck this is a true blessing from God and the fine people from the Isle of Islay.

When Admiral Schnuck got back on the line with Carver Mettle he was almost gleeful. "I should be fine in the next hour or so. . . Achoo, Achoo . . . Achoo . . . Achoo."

"Admiral, I'm sure it will work for you as it has for me. Now let me tell you what I am going to do about this man named Clement Athelwhite."

❋

Clement Athelwhite sat in his small office in Geneva. The slim, six-foot-three, New Zealander with sandy hair had no axe to grind, or so it seemed. He had been annoyed that calls were coming to him from Carver Mettle, from the United Nations.

"Why would you espouse that Ubi Ubi should be jailed?" the voice mail from Mettle asked. "What is the reason for your interest in subduing Premier Ubi. What has he done to create this animus? The country of Ubi is not fair game for international politics. It has not done anything but to keep the peace during its 24 years of existence, only to promulgate the eefer medicine and herbs that have helped millions of people to a better existence."

Athelwhite was afraid to answer the voice mail, afraid to explain his stance and his imploring of the World Health Organization to put a crimp into Premier Ubi's industry. He was also anxious to not cross spurs with Gilly Gigli and the powerful E.H. Meris Co., who had urged him to take action against Ubi and his country. Gilly and his liege, Bobbe Birstein, had made it clear that it was time to put Premier Ubi at bay, to reconstruct the way the eefer seeds were produced and distributed for the rest of the world. Athelwhite would not pleased to have to return a $10 million deposit in his name in the Credit Swisse bank account opened for him by Gilly.

✵

"Clement Athelwhite has been with the W.H.O since 1986. He has a stellar record as a diplomat, if only a high-level functionary," Carver Mettle told Admiral Schnuck. "But he has operated businesses on the side and these are businesses that have rung up a string of debts to the tune of $5 million. Our U.N. investigators say he was ripe for the money that Gilly Gigli apparently advanced him, and, of course, Gigli knew that. Gigli was looking for the Achilles heel in Athelwhite and he certainly found it."

"Well, what can we do to take the onus off of Premier Ubi and place it upon Clement Athelwhite?" asked Admiral Schnuck.

"I am still having trouble proving the transaction between Gilly Gigli and Clement Athelwhite, but when I can do that your Premier will undoubtedly go Scot free. Our investigators are moving forward and I think this will be easy to prove. Until then, one must assume that Ubi Ubi is guilty of the cartel and illegal activities he will be charged with in Chile," said Mettle, being careful not to offer Admiral Schnuck any glimpse of immediate hope until there was a greater degree of evidence in Ubi Ubi's favor as opposed to findings against Athelwhite.

"How revolting that Premier Ubi has to endure time in a jail cell until all this is resolved," said Admiral Schnuck. "You don't know Premier Ubi... he has the moral compass of a saint."

"All I know is that the United Nations will neither tolerate improper activity by Premier Ubi any more than it will accept what could be a plot between Athelwhite and the E. H. Meris Co.," said Carver Mettle in the typical ambivalence of the career public servant that he is.

"We will be the judge of who is right and who is wrong," said Mettle, not too convincingly.

❀

CHAPTER TWENTY-FIVE

Christian And Columbus Are Hot On The Trail Of Artha's Killer

As SPIRALS OF UBIANS MARCHED 15 and 20 deep around the Ubi Marriott and four blocks down the street at the Ubi Club, the Fung Hi region, noted for its placidity, had erupted into a chanting, ominous resolve of human force.

It was the second day of the revolt and lock-in of the two buildings, both of which housed the representatives of the E.H. Meris Co., the lawyers form the Holy See and Smiley Watkins and his gang of real estate interests. Inside the buildings, the inhabitants were beginning to show a restlessness, yet each group continued to plot its way to victory. Some, like Gigli Gilly, head of E.H. Meris, thought the lock-in an amusement wherein he could actually better direct his battle to take over the eefer tree production. He had all of his key players' undivided attention. Bobbe Birstein had gone over to the Ubi Club the morning before to caucus with Gilly and Genny Chancellor had already been there, as he was consorting with Father Crosetti in Crosetti's suite there. Bobbe tracked Chancellor down on his cell phone, and for the last day and a half, Gigli Gilly's capacious suite had become their war room.

Their colleague, Sheryl Chan, was locked up inside the Marriott but they had all been in contact until this afternoon, the second day of the revolt, when the cell phones ceased working because the electricity had been turned off and there was no way to re-charge them. Phone lines had been cut off the first day. All this gave Sheryl pause to think about some things.

For one, she was annoyed with Platsy Schmid, who had come down to Ubi as part of a growing Meris entourage the week before. Gilly wanted as many of his best people around him, and Platsy, the 44-year-old heir to the Meris throne, certainly was at the top of the list.

Of course, he wished to visit with her and he did. They had made love in her suite at the Marriott on two nocturnal occasions, the last of which left her empty and aggrieved. She called him the next day and suggested that the relationship best be platonic going forward. Egoist that he is, Platsy was not happy with her decision. There weren't many good looking professional women staying at the Marriott and he'd really have to work his wiles on them, when he had had Sheryl in his pocket, or so he thought. He doubtfully could find anyone as attractive and bright to spend his time with. This isn't Bern or Geneva or Paris, he thought, where the beautiful women hang from trees for the picking like the eefer seeds do here.

"Sheryl, my lovely Sheryl, I vish that you vill reconsider," said Platsy Schmid. "Vee've got a lot going on together. The two of us together can take control of Meris and run it as vee vant, the most majestic business couple on the planet. Vee'll be famous together. Vee'll be in Fortune magazine, even People. Vee'll be on television like movie stars. Please reconsider."

"No, at least not now, Platsy," said Sheryl directly. "This is a critical time for the company and I think we should put other considerations to the side and work toward our goals of commanding the eefer seed market. Besides, we need to cool it down. Neither one of us knows where our connection would lead us. Neither one of us is ready for any sort of commitment, especially you."

"You disappoint me, Sheryl," said Platsy. "You truly disappoint me. Vee've had such good times together.

"Can't vee have at least conjugal visits vhile vee are marooned down here in Ubi?" he continued. "Vee are so good together, you know that my love."

Sheryl, who now found him pathetic and almost sniveling, intoned, "Look, the past is the past. I have no interest in continuing anything. We have the ability to be colleagues but that is going to have to be it. You'll find somebody else, and quickly I'm sure... all the nubile girls go for you and you have the roving eye. Let's just be friends.

Jimmy Christian had just delivered two bottles of Bunnahabhain to Admiral Schnuck, which the Admiral thought would cure his sudden curse of the sneezes. After a few gulps neat, rather psychologically or truly physically, the Admiral ceased achooing and felt much better too.

During the visit to the Petite Palais offices of the Admiral, Jimmy Christian gave him an update on the progress toward finding the person or persons who murdered Artha Crowder.

"The funny thing, boss, is that whoever killed Artha is locked into the Ubi Club or the Marriott. That could be any of 20 people as I see it. Dennis Columbus, you know, Dennis Columbus, the private investigator from New York, is helping us. He and I and Caz Caswell and Densmore Assault have really been on this caper for the past week and I think we have some likely culprits, and we can prove it."

"Tell me more, tell me more… achoo, achoo," said the Admiral.

"Bless you, Admiral. We discovered two Cuban cigars, Romeo & Julietta's, in the inside pocket of Artha's suit coat when we got his clothes back from the coroner's office. One of them had teeth marks on it and had been smoked a little. We all know Artha didn't smoke, would never smoke and basically couldn't stand smoke," Jimmy said in his deep, husky voice caused in part by the fact that he had smoked three packs of cigarettes a day up until a few years ago. "Man, this just doesn't jibe."

"Jimmy, I can't even believe Artha would accept cigars, not even to give to someone else who smokes them. He so despised them," said Admiral Schnuck, his sneezing beginning to simmer down noticeably.

"We think it was an afterthought, an absent-minded mistake by the killer or killers. And we think Artha Crowder may have even been dead before he was hung from eefer tree "A," stated Jimmy.

"Unfortunately, based on that, just about anyone from overseas who is here right now could be the killer," Jimmy Christian continued. "They all smoke cigars, but not too many of us Ubians do. Hell, even the big shots like Gilly Gigli, Father Crosetti, Smiley Watkins… I think even Cabby

Thomas and those guys... they all smoke cigars. So do their little wiener henchmen. I even saw that Chinese girl from Meris smoking a cigar at O'Fabo's last week. And Dennis Columbus saw a hot tamale Brazilian woman out with Cabby Thomas, and she was smoking cigars, too. And every one of the yuppies visiting the Marriott or the Ubi Club or my place all smoke cigars."

"Oh, my. This looks like a rat's nest of the first order," said the Admiral.

"Not, as bad as you think, Admiral. A box of Romeo y Julietta's was delivered to the front desk of the Ubi Club the day before Artha was found murdered. And we know who it was delivered to," said Jimmy.

"But that can't possibly determine a killer, can it, Jimmy?"

"No, Admiral Schnuck, but that person may be someone we want to talk to."

"Who is that person?"

"That person is Father Crosetti, the Vatican lawyer."

"Holy Bee-Jesus!"

❋

CHAPTER TWENTY-SIX

How The People Who Are Locked In Are Reacting

It was growing increasingly stifling inside the Marriott and down the street at the Ubi Club. Outside, marchers continued around the clock and were usually 10 or 12 deep as they picketed the buildings. They would come in shifts of every six hours. Replacements would keep the energy steady, chanting in a drone that was as mystifying as it was suffocating.

TV crews and other international media were camped out up and down the streets of Fung Hi. There was even a stand of risers to accommodate the television crews on Abdidli Street, across from the Ubi Club. Yes, this was becoming the global story that the Ubians and their leaders had hoped for.

The fervor of the Ubians had grown in this the second day of Premier Ubi Ubi's imprisonment in Chile, and they had two goals: one, to see that he is released and, two, that they would force the oppressors to go home, to leave Ubi for good. They wanted their Premier back in Ubi and they wanted their country to return to the peaceful mode that had made it the envy of other nations around the world.

In an interview with Bernard Shaw from CNN, Shif-Lee Ubi explained his country's cause as best he could. Being the 25-year-old Interior Minister for his country and also the son of Ubi Ubi was not easy.

"Mr. Shaw, you can see from the peaceful demonstrations around these buildings that our people are well-intentioned. We have two primary reasons for conducting this demonstration and they are, first, to cause the people who wish to possess our land for their own purposes to reconsider; second, to bring a clear awareness to the problems Ubi faces and what we hope to do about them. And, I might add, that we hope to shift public opinion around the world into our court so that we will gain support from the United Nations, the World Rights Foundation and the World Health Organization.

"The power of the eefer seed as a processed medicine and herb was discovered here in Ubi, the only place on earth where the eefer trees grow in abundance. It was handed down from older generations of my father's family and then developed by him and his associated partners from smaller pharmaceutical firms around the world into what many are referring today as the 'miracle drug' of the 21st century. Now we are facing predators who want to take away the eefer business from us or take our land or both. We are a small country by most standards, Mr. Shaw, but we are proud of our heritage and our people who call themselves Ubians. Let me remind the United Nations, the media and all concerned people around the world that we have been a model country, one which has comported itself with kindness and understanding toward its citizens and everyone else. We have done so without a court system, without lawyers and without arcane politics for almost 25 years. My father is the architect of the Ubian culture and the developer of the country as we know it today. I must make it clear that he is so wrongly imprisoned in Chile. We do not wish him or our citizens to be victimized by our own success. And we do not wish to be taken advantage of in any way. We ask the world to come to our defense and see the logic in our position."

Shif-Lee had graduated to a new maturity in his comments and showed strong signs of leadership in other live interviews with Dan Rather and Tom Brokaw and earlier with Peter Jennings. He stood in front of the cameras and held his own and back in Punta Arenas Chile, his mother Takita watched the CNN report from her hotel room, proud that she was witnessing the emergence of a young man who she could see had many traits and signs of the wisdom of his father.

The same was true in interviews he gave with The New York Times, The London Times, The Washington Post and Japan's Yomiuri Shimbun, among the other chroniclers of international events.

❄

In Chile, Taki had heard the knock on the door and presumed it would be the Belgian Ambassador, Yrral Lieber. It was, and the news that he was bringing was not what she wanted to hear.

"I've talked with the Punta Arenas chief of police and the arresting captain from the state police and they seem to be hand-tied without the completion of the paperwork coming from the World Health Organization," he said. "The Chilean state police are holding control of the disposition of Premier Ubi. Their officials will meet with the World Rights Foundation tomorrow, and I'm afraid that would be the earliest Premier Ubi could be released. I am also talking by phone with our own delegation to the United Nations in New York and our Washington embassy to see what help they can give."

He continued, "The better news, Mrs. Ubi, is that the Premier is in good spirits in spite of his confinement. They are not allowing him to view television but I have filled him in on what positive comments are coming through the news media. I said your son is doing a good job of making the world understand the plight of Premier Ubi and his country. He was gleaming when I left him. I just want you to know that he is doing well, and I hope this all will be over soon."

"Thank you Yrral, you are a good friend to Premier Ubi and his family," said Taki. Yrral Lieber put his hand on Taki's right knee and gave it an ample squeeze.

The Ubian demonstrators allowed guests with proper credentials to leave the Ubi Club and the Ubi Marriott. The leaders of the demonstration and lock-in were careful to not allow anyone from the Holy See lawyer group, the E.H. Meris Co., or the Smiley Watkins development crew to leave the buildings. Anyone else with the right identification could leave the buildings and virtually everybody did, because this the second day of the lock-in found the buildings anything but hospitable, without the air conditioning and all power and water turned off and no means of communicating with the outside world.

Some of those locked in actually were having a pretty good time, especially Cabby Thomas, the golf course architect, and his new friend, Lachitcha Lasos, one of the world's great porn stars. It was hot in Cabby's junior suite on the 19th floor of the Marriott, but that didn't seem to bother them a bit. They had no food, except for what was left in the Bartech automatic refreshment center in the room. There was still some booze and juices left in the Bartech and centrally they were having a good time. Cabby figured he was only an innocent bystander in all that was going on, and he'd probably leave the next day, with fond memories of the girl of his dreams intact and the promise of a long-lasting relationship with her.

Actually, the demonstrators planned to let their oppressors out as soon as the three groups could come to an agreement that they should leave. The Ubians were not about to let one group go and the others stay. This would not be a squatters' rights situation by any means. The nearly four dozen people holed up in the Ubi Club and the Marriott from the three different oppressing groups had to all go at once, according to the edict of Shif-Lee Ubi and carried out by his direct aides. There would be no negotiation or any sort of dialogue with the three groups and the Ubians. Simply put, they could be released from their "imprisonment" when all three parties would leave at once. At that point, they would be shuttled to the Ubi International Airport, under guard, and presumably sent back to their respective countries, agreeing never to return to the land of Ubi.

Shif-Lee figured they'd all give out by the third or fourth days and then the siege would be over and life in Ubi could return to the pleasant way it was meant to be.

Smiley Watkins and his colleagues, save for Cabby Thomas, continued to meet in Watkins' suite, working on the drawings and plans for the golf courses, hotels and residential communities. And, Watkins was working up a "deal" that he wanted to offer Premier Ubi for the land, an offer, Smiley thought, that the old man couldn't refuse.

Meanwhile, Gilly Gigli refused even the thought of giving up his intentions of taking control of the eefer production on a worldwide basis. He was stymied, however, by the fact that he had no way of communicating back home to his headquarters in Bern, Switzerland. But he continued to caucus with Bobbe Birstein, Genny Chancellor and Platsy Schmid. He couldn't reach Sheryl Chan because she was locked in the Marriott and the four men in the Ubi Club. After Platsy got drop-kicked out of Sheryl Chan's room, he had gone over to the Ubi Club to see Gilly and that is where he has been since the first day of the lock-in. There was one king-size bed in Gilly's suite and that is where the four would take turns napping. Sometimes though more than one of them would squeeze onto the bed, a giant canopy bed with long, scrolled posters, for some shut-eye. When he could, Genny Chancellor would sneak down to Father Crosetti's room at the other end of the "L"-shaped corridor on the fourth floor of the Club. Poor Platsy was pining for Sheryl Chan, but there wasn't a way for him to see her, and even if there were, she wouldn't have seen him.

The other brigade of people from the Church, from E. H. Meris and from Smiley Watkins' operations were pretty much cordoned in the Marriott, save for Crosetti's two priest/ secretaries who were stationed at the Ubi Club to be handy for his beck and call like two androgynous handmaidens. While he had little alcohol or any kind of beverage or food left to digest, Augustino Crosetti did have a good dozen and a half Cuban cigars remaining to while away his time. And it was this contemplation with puffs of blue smoke that led him to hatch a plan that he thought made the most sense in his mission to wrestle away the country from the 24-year

regime of Premier Ubi   Ubi.   He decided to take a walk
down the hall and pay Gilly Gigli a visit.

❋

CHAPTER TWENTY-SEVEN

A Breakthrough
For Ubi Ubi

Takita Salernas del Rios-Ubi heard the phone ring in her suite at the Hotel Jose Nogueira. She knew it could only be one person, Yrral Lieber, the Belgian ambassador to Chile. He was the only one who had her private number at the hotel. Taki was somewhat taken aback at the odd way Ambassador Lieber had embraced her knee the previous day after bringing her up to date on the developments concerning her husband. Maybe he was just a horny, lusty, aging middle-aged man who found her attractive, she thought. Maybe this was simply the Belgian way. She knew this, however: he might be her only hope of getting through the cobweb of bureaucracy that was keeping Ubi Ubi in the Punta jail.

"Taki, I have good news this morning," said Lieber. "The men from the World Rights Foundation have met with the chief of police and officials from the state police and it appears Premier Ubi should be let go some time this afternoon. The United Nations has stepped in and the indications are that there were some irregularities in the order to arrest your husband, and the grounds are highly dubious. But, moreover, I have received a call from Hanover Simpson, the former President of the United States, and he wishes to step into the stalemate with the lock-in in Ubi and also ensure that your husband is released from jail."

Taki breathed a sigh of relief upon hearing these words. Her husband had already been in the Punta jail for more than two days and now it was the third day. She never thought that she could be so happy to leave her home country of Chile, but she wanted to go as soon as the Premier was released from jail.

"Thank you Yrral," she said. "What will happen next?"

"Ubi seems to have a good friend in Carver Mettle of the United Nations," said the Ambassador. "He has been in touch with your chief of staff, Admiral Schnuck, and with Hanover Simpson and all three are in agreement that Ubi Ubi was wrongfully arrested last Friday. He'll be in jail three days but I don't think a day after that. In fact, Hanover Simpson wants to come to Chile and pick the two of you up tomorrow in his private Gulfstream jet. I have a surprise for you as well."

"What is that?" asked Taki. "Will he take us back to Ubi?"

"No, not right away. We don't think it will be safe yet. No, Simpson wants to take both of you to New York City, to the United Nations. I don't know if you're aware, but just this moment in New York nearly 200 world leaders are meeting in an unprecedented conclave about world peace and other matters. These include monarchs, presidents, prime ministers and premiers.

"I'm afraid the country of Ubi was overlooked when the invitations went out but with all the press your nation is receiving at this time, and because of what it has represented for so long, the U.N. officials think it would be appropriate to invite Premier Ubi to speak before this delegation. Just about everyone is there. Even people who don't get along with one another, such as those from the Middle East and some parts of Africa.

"They are planning a remarkable, historic photo of the leaders and they want to include Ubi Ubi. The picture of these kings and other national leaders will be displayed in newspapers all over the world."

"Ambassador Lieber, I can't believe what a turnabout there has been in our fortunes in the last 24 hours," said Taki.

"Well, let me say, Hanover Simpson believes the two of you will walk into the United Nations with him as international heroes, icons if you will for the very purpose of this meeting," said Lieber.

"Hanover Simpson may be in the movie business today, but he hasn't forgotten how to be a statesman. Some of this is obviously politically and ego motivated, but it certainly cannot hurt Premier Ubi and yourself. It might even help the former President sell some of his movie projects. Nothing like finding a singular way to be in the public's mind's eye, is there, Taki?"

"If things work out the way I think, I will personally deliver Premier Ubi back to your hotel later in the afternoon. Then we should have a little celebration, don't you think?"

"Yes, yes, Yrral. I thought our world was crumbling around us the last few days. You moved so fast in correcting these injustices. Now, to have an opportunity to address the United Nations about our plight – against those evil predators who want to take our country from us – will clearly gain the ear of many other nations," she said.

"The media have already brought much attention to your battle against the insurgents," said the Ambassador. "Premier Ubi's talk before the United Nations will be the frosting on the cake. Hanover Simpson wants to introduce the two of you before the entire delegation in the Grand Assembly Hall the day after tomorrow, the last day of the conference."

"Now that Ubi Ubi is being released from jail, we must work on returning our country to order and removing from it its sources of agony," said Taki. "This afternoon we can cheer getting my husband back to me, and at the same time we must toast our affirmation to returning Ubi to the Ubians."

As promised by Yrral Lieber, Premier Ubi Ubi was released from the Punta Arenas jail that afternoon. Ambassador Lieber picked him up at the jail in his chauffer-driven Mercedes and immediately headed for the Hotel Jose Nogueira for a toast.

When they got there and Taki opened the door to the suite she was radiant, easily looking 20 years younger than her 56 years. She gave Ubi Ubi a warm hug and kiss, as Ambassador Lieber leered. The three of them toasted quietly with some top shelf pisco, some cheeses and cantelope.

"I look forward to seeing you both in Ubi, once things have settled down there. My assistant, Bretta Schiffna, would like to join me on that visit," said Lieber, with a hearty smirk only a true reprobate like him could wear. But what the heck, he got Ubi out of jail, didn't he? Why shouldn't he have some fun with his 29-year-old Croatian secretary?

❋

CHAPTER TWENTY-EIGHT

Hanover Simpson Arrives
On The Gulfstream

THE PUNTA ARENAS AIRPORT was crowded with the summer-time tourists, many of them going to the National Forest and other places in Patagonia. It is not a very large airport, so the gleaming white Gulfstream transoceanic jet stood out prominently on the tarmac, in between the LanChile and Ladeco commercial aircraft.

As the former President strode down the midships stairs of the Gulfstream, he was preceded by "Huey" and followed by "Duey," his two favorite Secret Service men, pals and fellow roustabouts. And after Duey came a knockout chick who bore a striking resemblance to Natalie Wood, and was, in fact, a bit of an actress. Simpson had met her during a casting meeting. Her name is Bathsheba Blakey and she is 32, an age when she knows she'll probably not make it as a box office bombshell but whose looks and body are well preserved and, well, just perfect for the 57-year-old Simpson. Her thigh-high scarlet mini and white satin blouse on her 5'4" frame called the eye's attention away from Simpson. And it was quite clear that the chest she was sporting came from one of the chi-chi doctors off Rodeo Drive.

The Ubies looked mesmerized as they waited at the gate for the Secret Service men to bring them out to the plane.

"Ubi and Takita, I cannot begin to explain how happy this day is for me," said Simpson. And now we can head to New York and see those boys at the U.N. Even Fidel Castro will be there, one of 180 leaders of countries from all over the world.

"Hey, let me introduce you to my special friend, Bathsheba. She's an actress really but more recently she has been helping me plan my two movie projects."

Bathsheba dutifully batted her dark eyes. Ubi looked amused. Taki somehow expected something like this. Well, it will be a long trip to Miami to stop for refueling and then on to New York. Conversation should be interesting. With Hanover Simpson, it would probably be a lot of listening, thought Taki, who in contrast to Bathsheba was wearing a dignified Chanel outfit of dark blue polka dots on cream.

"Hey, I got us two great suites on the 38th floor of the Pierre Hotel. Almost at the top! The best hotel in New York for my money. A lot of people live there permanently, but the hotel makes these suites available for its regular guests on upgrade. We'll have fun, after all the two of you have been through."

Bathsheba nodded bashfully, her red lipstick shimmering like a red lollipop. Her inflated cleavage indicated she must go to a tanning studio or perhaps she just sun bathed nude in the back garden of Simpson's suite at the Bel Air Hotel. No apparent lines.

On board the plane, Simpson's crew included a maid and a bartender/jack of all trades. The crew, including the pilots, seemed to genuinely like the former President. For being the ex head of state of the most powerful country in the world, Simpson had a fine facility for poking fun at himself and others. Ubi had to admit he is always fun to be around, though Ubi knew that beyond the happy-go-lucky exterior is a driven man who would think nothing of copping as much attention for himself as possible. Simpson didn't care that his girlfriend grabbed some of the attention away from him because he knew that Bathsheba was part of his entire package. He thought she enhanced his very presence, and he just might have been right.

Bathsheba who was busy looking at maps after take-off, remarked, rather amazingly, how Chile and California looked alike and how Chile, however, was much farther east than people thought. She noted that that the Pacific coast of Chile was about as far east as New York, when you looked at the map. She was right. "I like to look at maps and I also like to do crossword puzzles, unless they're real hard," she said to no one in particular as she sipped a pisco sour, while the former President lit up a Churchill-Padron cigar, offering Ubi Ubi one too.

The main thing, Taki thought, is that "we are on our way." She never recalled being so happy to leave her homeland. Really, Ubi was her home, even though she maintained Chilean citizenship. She knew it wasn't her hometown police or even the state police who should be blamed for Ubi Ubi's incarceration. The blame, she thought, rested solely on Gilly Gigli and probably Father Crosetti, somehow, but probably not so much on Smiley Watkins, who, from what she had heard, was a borderline country bumpkin with a mouth that was more dangerous than his ability to hurt anyone.

Bathsheba asked Taki if she had ever had a mud bath at the Bel Air Hotel. Taki said no. In fact, she said, she had never been to the Bel Air Hotel but that she heard it was very nice based on her husband's experiences there.

Bathsheba told Taki that she had read every John Grisham book ever published. She also had read all of the Mary Higgins Clark books. The only real old book she had read was Jack Kerouac's "On The Road." She said she hated the comic strips and actually rarely read newspapers, but she knew all about what was going on in Ubi because she thought Matt Lauer was sexy and she watched him on the Today Show.

Now the former President was squeezing her shoulders close to him. He was having a very good time and it showed. They'd be in New York by 9:30 p.m., and he was looking forward to the dinner he had arranged for the two couples. This would be at Sistina's, one of the city's finest Italian restaurants. He loved the lamb there. He loved the Northern Italian pasta dishes. And he knew he would love this visit to the Pierre Hotel, too. Batsheba had never been to the Pierre. He thought they'd both be in for a treat, high above Central Park East, at 61st Street.

Meanwhile, Ubi continued to take down notes for his address before the United Nations. He was just blocking out some ideas. He didn't want to read the speech, but he did want it to have a beginning, a middle and an end, so that all important points would not be forgotten. They were well over the Atlantic now and Taki, tired from all the turmoil of the past week was sound asleep.

After dinner that night, the four, under the mindful eyes of Huey and Duey, returned to the Pierre for after-dinner drinks at the Pierre Bar, maybe the best neighborhood bar in the world, in one of the best hotels, a hotel that has a European regality to it. Kathleen Landis, who has been at the Pierre for more than a decade, sang and played show tunes and popular jazz on the piano, while guests mingled in and out of the narrow bar room. Some were in Tuxedos from the usual nightly events and special dinners that take place in the hotel. In the Rotunda, up the stairs from the bar, were seated Jean Kirkpatrick and Henry Kissinger, the two former Secretaries of State. And across from them was the daytime soap opera star and recent, finally, emmy winner Susan Lucci.

Simpson and the Ubies had walked through the Rotunda to get to the bar and Simpson introduced Kirkpatrick and Kissinger to the Ubies. They knew Ubi Ubi would be talking to the United Nations and wished him well. An observer would not have known if either Kirkpatrick or Kissinger thought much of Simpson. The scene was cordial but not much more. One wondered if this had to do with Bathsheba's hanging on his right arm. She wore an Annie Hall hat and a flowing monk-like tunic of a blue-grey nature. Taki wore a smart black on black dress and black pumps.

When they got to the Pierre Bar it was quite crowded but a glass table, not a large table, was reserved for them. Huey and Duey stood near the bar and watched.

One thing could be said about Bathsheba. She was a trouper. She ordered the same Hine cognac that Simpson and Ubi had decided upon. Taki opted for a Spanish coffee.

Kathleen Landis played and sang some Gershwin and Porter and it seemed Hanover Simpson thought she had dedicated "You're the Top" just to him. He was pleased.

He toasted Ubi Ubi and said that at 9 a.m. tomorrow the 180-plus assembled leaders of the world would begin to know a lot more about Ubi from its founder. Simpson was pleased that, even though he was no longer in office, he would have the opportunity to introduce Ubi Ubi on the floor of the Great Hall of the U.N.

At 57, Simpson showed no signs of tiredness, even though it was now 12:23 a.m. and the four of them had completed a 14-hour flight that day, leaving very early in the morning from Chile. The Ubies decided to retire for the night and left Simpson with Bathsheba, both of whom had one more Hine before going upstairs. Simpson rather liked being seen out with the young lady. She is different, he thought, to the extent that people notice her; then, he thought, they look up and notice him and, he thought, they'd say "well, I'll be darn, look who's over there." He liked that a lot.

❀

CHAPTER TWENTY-NINE

Things Are Reaching
A Boil In Ubi

ON TOP OF THE FACT THAT the souls in the Ubi
Club and the Ubi Marriott were getting toasty from the heat,
the lack of food and drink and the inability to communicate
to the outside world, strange things were happening in the
air. Outside, winds kept percolating in different swirls, the
skies turned a purple haze and red, and taller than usual
waves lapped up upon the soft pink sands of the Ubian
beaches.

"We're in for one hell of a storm," said Jimmy Christian
to Dennis Columbus and Caz Caswell and Felonius Assault.
The latter three had gathered early at Jimmy's bar to discuss
the progress on finding Artha Crowder's killer and to be
brought up to date on the pressing developments of the
demonstrations and lock-in.   Soon after, Admiral Robert
Peter Schnuck and Shif-Lee Ubi gathered there as well.

"Premier Ubi is going to address the United Nations
tomorrow," said Admiral Schnuck. "By then it will be well
into the fourth day of the revolt and the lock-in and if we
haven't driven the beasts out of their hovels and into the

streets for deportation out of the country I don't know what will. They've got to be at the breaking point."

As the winds picked up, Jimmy went over to close some shutters on the windows at O'Fabo's. In the last hour the temperature had dropped from 85 to 68 and seemed to continue to fall.

O'Fabo's is just a mere block away from the shore and it was easy to hear the waves lapping hard against the jetty at the center of the Ubian portside. Nonetheless, the people by the thousands continued to march around the Ubi Club and the Ubi Marriott down Abdidli Street in Fung Hi.

Jimmy and Dennis told Admiral Schnuck that they thought it might be a good idea to go over to the Ubi Club and the Marriott to interview some of the foreigners, people they thought might have a link to the murder of Artha Crowder. In particular, Dennis, the Private-I from Manhattan, wanted to spend some time with Father Augustino Crosetti. He wanted to know how it was that two of his cigars had ended up in the inside suit jacket pocket of Artha Crowder. Dennis figured that these were cigars from Crosetti because Romeo y Julietta's Cubans were not sold in Ubi, though they can be special ordered. And that is exactly what Crosetti had done, having them delivered last week to the Ubi Club from Switzerland.

"You folks seem to be making good progress on Artha's killing," said Admiral Schnuck. "I do hope you identify the killer before we force these people out of Ubi. Once they're gone we'll have a damned hard time convincing anyone in the outside world that any of them should be convicted. Whoever it is will get off Scot-free."

"Don't worry about that," answered Dennis Columbus. "I think the killer might reveal himself in the next day. We'll force his hand, or have someone else spill the beans on him. It think it is imminent."

❀

The clouds continued to darken in the late afternoon. Even, the tall, stately eefer trees were bending like bows in the wind. Some of the Ubian demonstrators were having trouble keeping their footing as the gale-force gusts just kept getting stronger. It seemed the inclement weather was a signal that this siege of principles against avarice was about to be broken.

In Gilly Gigli's suite at the Ubi Club, Father Crosetti was sitting with sweat pouring down his forehead. He would wipe his brow with his handkerchief every other moment. He shared a cigar with Gilly as Gilly's men, Birstein and Chancellor and Schmid, looked on. Also attending the discussion were Crosetti's two priest/secretaries, who said nothing, just took notes, expressionless with flat, tight lips. They might as well have been nuns.

Gigli and Crosetti held the stage, their demeanor being oddly similar. These were men who were used to getting there way with things. And they were dealmakers.

"I get the impression that you don't like me very much Mr. Gigli," said the priest and lawyer. "You haven't been very friendly since our first introduction early last week. And perhaps I don't wish to be at all fond of you, but I can tell you here and now we are at an impasse. Those clowns outside want us to give in and get out. That could cost us all everything we are seeking. I am at a point that I don't give one hell of a damn whether Ubi Ubi gets one lousy centime for his land, which rightfully is ours. And, I bet, neither do you. But the trouble, Mr. Gigli, is that we are also fighting each other for the spoils, and I was thinking yesterday that maybe we should find a way to split them between us. We might even split in that disgusting fat pervert Smiley Watkins, because we want the eefer business and all he wants is to build golf courses, hotels and condominiums. We need those kinds of things here, if we expect people to visit Fung Hi, which is what I would suggest changing the whole country's name to when we take over. The name Ubi is anathema to me and should be to you as well.

"In fact I'll tell you that the Holy See would be plenty happy to just lease this all to both of you and take a percentage of business on top of that. What do you think?" Crosetti asked in his impeccable English, just one of six languages he had mastered in his work as a world-class lawyer for the Holy See.

"You present an interesting thought process," said Gigli. "Frankly, I am ready to get out of this godforsaken place and go home vhere I have my paradise. It is time to make a move. Though I haven't seen anything from the news media since they browned us out here, my suspicion is that people are starting to single out E.H. Meris as an evil pursuer of eefer. Vee're big business and everybody likes to hate us for the littlest of reasons. Perhaps if vee team up vee'll diffuse the attention - spread it around. If vee put simple Smiley Watkins into the equation vee'll diffuse everything even more. Vhat vee're saying is that this country called Ubi vill be made into a multi-use land – an alliance of people using it for different purposes."

"Exactly, right," said Crosetti. "Look, the Church is into real estate; we don't necessarily operate that real estate, rather we like to own it. You people want production out of the eefer trees, so be it. Watkins wants the glitz and golf. Let's do all three. The thing we have to do next is try to get to the Texan so that we can present a unified force. And that is not easily done considering that we are locked into this tomb."

Suddenly, Platsy Schmid piped in. "Look, I can try to find a vay to get out of here and run over to the Marriott to talk to Smiley Vatkins. I haven't met him, but I know a lot about him from Sheryl Chan," he said, thinking he could kill two birds with one stone if he could get over to the Marriott. Platsy could not accept the rejection Sheryl had given him, and, being Platsy the playboy, he always saw hope."

"Vell, I don't know how you vill go undetected, but that vill be up to you," said Gilly, glowering at Platsy's comrades, Birstein and Chancellor. "These other two von't take the initiative. That's vhy you are the fair-haired boy in our company. You have balls."

Platsy wasn't sure either how he would find his way out of the Ubi Club and over to the Marriott to talk with Smiley Watkins. But he didn't get this far at Meris without being a slippery devil. This was the kind of challenge that Platsy relished, and he'd come home a hero once again.

Platsy looked out the window from Gilly Gigli's suite and began to think that the rotten weather out there might just be his ally.

Downstairs, a number of the marchers had broken ranks, only because it was starting to rain sideways and the winds were belching vigorously as the skies darkened though the sun would not set for another couple of hours.

Group leaders were already transporting the older Ubians up into the highlands area of Ubi, the hilly, almost mountainous region, above the eefer tree line and naturally protective from the surging elements. Once, about 20 years ago, Ubi was hit by monstrous, hurricane-force storms. The hills there have a dense jungle of thick vegetation that served as protection from overhead rains. It was thought that this natural encampment provided security centuries ago along the opposite side of the hills, which kept the marauders from China and Mongolia from taking control of the peoples residing in the low lands. Thus, the hills and overhead folliage protected the people from the vicissitudes of the sea and the vagaries of the most deleterious notions of the human spirit.

Shif-Lee Ubi, the interior minister, was most aware of this protection as he worried about the wellbeing of the Ubians marching around the buildings to secure the lock-in of the oppressing forces.

In a conversation with Admiral Schnuck later that day, Shif-Lee and the Admiral were carefully making plans for an evacuation of Ubi's citizenry if the weather conditions continued to worsen. They also put a call into Premier Ubi's suite at the Pierre in New York to alert him of the conditions and bring him up to speed on the revolt and lock-in prior to his meeting with the United Nations later that morning.

"Please don't take any chances," Ubi told them. "The weather is a portent of something ominous."

❋

CHAPTER THIRTY

Ubi Ubi Addresses The United Nations

NEW YORK CITY WAS IN A state of pure gridlock by 7 a.m. the morning Premier Ubi was to address the United Nations. And like in the nation of Ubi, it was raining - hard.

Former President Simpson's limo had picked him and Premier Ubi and Taki up on the 5th Avenue side of the hotel and they began making their way to the U.N. on 1st Avenue, only blocks away on the east side, but traffic was slowed to a crawl with the influx of the more than 180 heads of state and their entourages.

As usual Hanover Simpson was in good spirits. Premier Ubi was too, though he wondered what the resolve would be ahead for his country and the trouble it was facing. He wondered just how much the U.N. would be on his side. And he worried about his country people and the storms that we're ceaselessly blowing onto the mainland.

Back at the hotel, Bathsheba slept well, content with a world that would allow her to bed down with the former

President of the United States, to her and many others an interesting, delightful, energetic man.

About an hour after they left the Pierre, Simpson and Premier Ubi arrived at the 46th entrance of the U.N., a complex that spreads from 42nd to 49th Streets on 1st Avenue. They alighted the gray stretch limo and were greeted by a half dozen Secret Service people. The President's personal guards, Huey and Duey, followed. Kofi Annan, the U.N. Secretariat General, had his chief of protocol greet the two chiefs of state and they were escorted to a private reception hall in the General Assembly section of the U.N. When they arrived in the reception hall they found Secretariat General Koffi Annan waiting for them along with 13 other U.N. officials.

Annan told Ubi Ubi that he had been following the events taking place in Ubi and said he thought the vast majority of delegates to the huge conclave of heads of state would be in favor of the actions the Ubians were implementing.

This made Ubi Ubi feel comfortable and more assured of the talk that he would make before the General Assembly in the next half hour. Hanover Simpson was happy as well, as he hadn't been back to the U.N. in the last four years since completing his term of President of the U.S.

As Annan and his aides talked with Premier Ubi, former President Simpson seemed to be pre-occupied with his visage reflected in a glass covered photo of Dag Hammersjold, the famed U.N. Secretariat General of the 1950s. It seemed as if Simpson was having a conversation with Hammersjold in the way the former President bobbed his head to one side and the other to make certain all strands of his fringe hair were in place and his red folard tie was knotted perfectly against his blue shirt with the white collar and French cuffing. He wore his standard navy double-breasted suit with a starched white pocket square jutting ever so elegantly from his left breast pocket. He seemed momentarily oblivious to the conversations in the room as he primped.

Ubi Ubi had on a Turnball & Asser rep tie against a white shirt framed in a single-breasted grey flannel suit. While Simpson was border-line foppish, Premier Ubi had the look of restrained elegance. And he was relaxed as he awaited the 9 a.m. start time of the General Assembly meeting this day.

Ubi did not wish any food from the regal buffet in the room.   He just sipped a grapefruit juice, while Simpson tore into a plump
croissant and grabbed some chocolate covered strawberries.

Outside horns blared and brakes screeched as New Yorkers funneled into their work places, many not understanding why this meeting of heads of state couldn't have been held over the Labor Day weekend instead of right after the holiday during the work week. Simpson did not seem to notice the cacophony; he was getting ready for his own remarks before the Assembly. Without a note.

Not many minutes later Simpson and Premier Ubi were escorted into the hall.   Inside and outside the cavernous building New York police and Secret Service people predominated. Never before had so many powerful leaders of the world gathered at the U.N. You could cut the security in and around the U.N. with a knife.   And even in the air above, government helicopters zoomed in spirals and heavy anti-attack vans and trucks covered the blocks between 49th and 42nd Streets.

And when Ubi Ubi strode down the main aisle in the great hall, led by Koffi Annan and Hanover Simpson, the crowd of imperials rose to their feet and offered a thundering hand clap sending chills down Ubi's spine. He had expected nothing like this, rather he thought they would just be seated. As he walked toward the podium, the applause continued and so did the smiles. Fidel Castro gave him a strong wink of the right eye, and Yasser Arafat crossed arms in the ritual Ubian gesture of greeting. And there was a roar of voices along with the clapping.

Ubi sat beside Annan on the podium as Simpson walked to the lectern. Simpson had not felt such a rush since the last time he addressed Congress in his State of the Union speech more than four years ago. Making pictures was fun, he thought, but nothing came close to this kind of adulation, though even he knew that much of it was in respect to Premier Ubi Ubi, who had started a country a quarter of a century ago and many years later had to defend himself and his nation against the plunderers who wished the land for themselves. Ubi recognized many of the prime ministers, presidents, premiers and monarchs and some he did not. What he did feel was an enveloping embrace from most everyone in the room, and he felt hope that the problems his country faced would soon become memories instead of realities. He smiled serenely as he looked out at his powerful admirers.

Simpson looked as if he were about to deliver the Gettysburg Address, pausing his comments noticeably until the roar died down.

"Gentlemen and ladies (there were only a handful of women heads of state present), I want to tell you how honored I am to be here as a former President of the United States of America. I served my country for eight full years, and I must tell you nothing gives me more pride than to have the opportunity today to introduce to you the David in the Golliath world of oppression. Ubi may be a very small country by most standards. It only occupies 24 square miles, but the people contained within it have a collective heart that we should all aspire to.

"This great meeting of the United Nations, perhaps a once in history undertaking, is dedicated to first and foremostly peace in the world, and I know you share with me the representation of that peaceable humanitarianism that we can glean from the country of Ubi and from its Premier, Ubi Ubi. We are so fortunate to have Premier Ubi in our presence, and I must add, why have we waited so long to acknowledge his works in the social consciousness that we should all embrace? Premier Ubi is no different from our own founding father, George Washington. He is no different from Abraham Lincoln or even Lyndon Baines Johnson. He is a leader with a mission and that mission is dedicated to making life secure and prosperous for his country men and women, many of whom have come from all corners of the world to live in Ubi and stay there for the generations to come.

"He is also no different from Martin Luther King or Pope John the 23rd. He has not a racist bone in his body and he loves deeply all peoples as should we all. When I see Fidel Castro and the Prime Minister of Topango embrassing warmly, I see hope. When I see the gleam of desire among those who have warred against each other in the Middle East and in Africa and in other parts of our world, I see hope. If we, gentlemen and ladies, have a crown jewel of inspiration for us all it is embodied in Premier Ubi Ubi and his country state's men and women. Someday our antecedents will look back upon this historic week and say, I hope and pray, this was the week that set the world on a new course of togetherness and gentility. And perhaps it is ironic and even mystical that this week was preceded by events that the whole world should find shameful, events that occurred in this promised land called Ubi. One of the most generous and decent men in the world was jailed because of some other people's pure and utter avarice. Some of the most gentle persons in the world were caused to demonstrate forcibly against oppression and literally fight for their right to live in a Camelot-like democracy perhaps unlike any we have seen in the history of the world. And I want you to know that I am Ubi Ubi's friend, I hope one of his best friends. From the moment I first met him in Ubi three months ago, I knew I had met one of the finest people in modern civilization. I only wish that each and every one of you could know Ubi like I know Ubi.

"I'm talking about the Premier Ubi you can play golf with, smoke a cigar with, fly long flights with and simply enjoy life with. And it is my distinct pleasure to introduce as well to you Mrs. Takita Ubi, the first lady of Ubi. Taki, will you please stand? Please let's all rise and recognize her." (Thunderous applause and whistles and another wink from Fidel Castro who is taken by this olive-skinned beauty.) Taki had not been at the earlier reception, but instead was invited to a brunch attended by the wives of the heads of state. This was a good thing, because the dramatic effect of introducing her now to the audience underscored the contentment Simpson exuded. He looked like a big canary who had just consumed some of the best bird seed available on the market today. He was more than pleased. And Fidel Castro winked at Taki once more.

What a wonderful experience. Rodney King was right when he wondered, "Why can't we just get along." Everybody was getting along here. Trading inside jokes, slapping each other on the back. Jews and Jordanians and Palestinians doing modified high fives.   Cheshire smiles. In a few weeks some of these revelers would be at odds with one another again.   But for now it was all sublime and Hanover Simpson seemed to be gushing in more than his share of credit.

He prattled on and on for another 20 minutes and then mercifully introduced Premier Ubi who then spoke to the Assembly.   Simpson's rambling filibuster of an intro lasted some 35 minutes, approximately 30 minutes longer than the speech of the man he introduced.

"Thank you, thank you, thank you," said Ubi to the Assembly.   "It is such an honor to be recognized by the leaders of our world. This is a red-letter day for my country and our people. Just a few days ago I was in a jail cell in Chile and I wasn't certain when I would be released. Just a few weeks ago we were deluged by ominous interests whose wish it is to take over our country, and to hell with the Ubians. You all have given my wife and me so much encouragement today. Our people are still demonstrating in our home land and they will continue to do so until we gain our goal, and that goal is to remove once and for all those people from outside who wish to take Ubi into their own hands for their own special interests.

"Ubi is just a little land to some people, but because of the far sweeping media coverage and the interest of countries throughout the world in our cause, we have gained a bit of fame in a way with which I believe many of you can identify. What has happened, indeed is happening in Ubi, could conceivably happen anywhere if any of us let our guards down.

"My dear friend, former United States President Hanover Simpson has come to our country's aide. I hope you each could have a friend like Hanover Simpson. He has another career now but for my money what he has done for my country is perhaps his most diplomatic act. When a career is ended as the President of the most powerful country in the world, a former President could wonder like Peggy Lee in her song, "Is That All There Is?" But President Hanover Simpson never wondered that. No, he took action, not for his own political gain because there was nothing to be gained, no office to seek; no, he just took it upon himself to lend a big hand of help. Nothing compelled him to do this other than the fact that he has a wonderfully warm heart and a feeling for his fellow man."

Ubi wasn't sure he fully believed in every aspect of his message to the Assembly, but he did appreciate that he probably wouldn't have had this audience without Simpson's fervent push. And as Ubi Ubi finished his remarks, he looked over to Hanover Simpson and he saw the expression of the Mona Lisa. Once more Hanover Simpson looked pleased. A few cynics in the Assembly were happy that they would not have to hear Simpson speak again to them any time soon.

When Simpson, Ubi and Taki returned to the Pierre with their security people in cars in front and behind them and Simpson's direct Secret Service men in the limo with them, they headed for the Pierre Bar, meeting Bathsheba. Joe, the tall Italian bartender and beverage director who has been a Pierre fixture for the past 25 years greeted them warmly. He knew the former President well but had not met his new girlfriend or the Ubies, but had heard about Simpson's and Ubi Ubi's address before the U.N. dignitaries on the radio that morning. He gave them his own quiet applause as they sat down at the bar. Joe is a guy who knows a lot of people from the four corners of the world, people who congregate at the Pierre Bar, some say the best neighborhood bar in the world. And he knows a lot about politics but is always discreet about the way he would parcel out opinions and information.

This was a good time to arrive at the Pierre Bar. It was about 12:30 p.m. and things were quiet. The rush of regulars would come in later in the afternoon to play liar's poker and to trade insults, as many of them had been doing for years. Investment bankers, brokers, lawyers, writers, pols. They perpetually exchange barbs, jokes and rumors but are all friends and Joe is at the center of all the repartee.

This was a good time to catch Joe, who was a terrific pitcher for Fordham University more than 40 years ago. He knows sports, several languages and talks easily on almost any topic. His uniform, like the Pierre, reflects a formality that certainly belies his ease with people.   This might as well be an exclusive version of the Love Boat, where your own personal bartender takes care of you in the manner of a century gone by. This was a good time to catch Joe because you pretty much had his undivided attention.

"Mr. President, so good to see you again. Your talk before the United Nations was terrific. I wish you were still in office," said Joe, as his big mitt grasped Hanover Simpson's hand.

"Joe, meet the one and only Ubi Ubi of Ubi and his wife Taki," said Simpson. "These are my dear friends and they have been through too much in the past few weeks. Let's get them each a big toddy. And this lovely lady is Batsheba. She's my friend from California."

Joe greeted both of the ladies placing his hands over their right hands and then he crossed his arms to recognize Premier Ubi Ubi in the customary Ubian manner. Premier Ubi looked pleased and returned the gesture. Joe is sharp that way.

Joe is about six-three and has a full head of slicked black hair. He is either in his late 50s or early 60s but looks much younger. His ruddy complexion and black hair, which may or may not be dyed, give him a pleasant look. Make no mistake, he runs his bar like a precious little fiefdom, directing his aides with hand signals and cracks in different languages, yet he smiles easily and is just as warm to the helpers as he is to his customers. Before he was at the Pierre, Joe tended bar at the Carleton House, kitty-corner across 61st Street from the Pierre. He and Norman, the tender at the Fatina Bar in the ever-name-changing hotel that used to be Westin that used to be the Ritz at 7th Avenue and 59th Street, could be the last of a breed. Customer friendly, great raconteurs, great greeters and people who have a facility for introducing strangers to strangers. And they say New York is unfriendly.

"What do you think will happen in your country after the revolt?" Joe asked Ubi. "I haven't seen this much coverage by the news media since the Middle East crisis in the early 1990s."

"Well, Joe, let me tell you that President Simpson is planning to fly us back to Ubi in the next few days," said the Premier. "Then, we hope, the uprising will be over and the people giving us so much trouble will have left the country and we can get back to having Ubi the way it was meant to be. I am glad the media are giving us so much attention over this disruption and I think virtually all of the coverage has been in our favor. Yet my wife and I will be so happy when all this is over. We are a quiet country that wishes to be independent, on its own. We wish to cause no one else any trouble, and in turn, we wish no trouble to befall ourselves."

"Premier Ubi, I can tell you that everyone I have talked to, who has come in here over the last few weeks, is in your favor," said Joe. "These aren't just our regulars from New York City but people from Germany, London, France, Spain, South America, Canada, Finland, from across the U.S., everywhere. People look at you as David against Goliath. They want you to win."

"Joey, Hanover and I can't wait to get to Ubi," said Bathsheba. "We have heard the beaches there are maybe the best in the world. Premier Ubi and Taki are going to have us stay at their home, the Petite Palais, which means the little palace in French, did you know that Joe?"

Joe has seen a lot of ditzes and bimbos in his life, but he just treats them like he would Princess Margaret. "No, I didn't know that. I wish I could go with you guys."

He looked at Taki and asked what the Petite Palais was like.

"Joe, it looks like a miniature version of your Monticello," she said. "Big columns in front. All white paint. A big lawn with gardens and many eefer trees surrounding the property. Everyone loves the Petite Palais. Inside, it is very woody - scrolled oaken paneled walls and walnut parquet floors.

"You'd really like our bird, Filigree, who makes himself the center of attention at the Petite Palais," she continued. "He probably talks more than any person who comes into your bar. We haven't seen him for almost two weeks. He's quite a card."

Joe had poured the four of them some Dom Perignon on the house, in honor of the victorious visit by Ubi Ubi to the heads of state at the United Nations. The roar of support as he and Hanover Simpson left the General Assembly hall was even greater than when they entered. And millions of people witnessed it on TV around the world. Certainly, it would seem that public opinion was gaining dramatically in favor of the Ubians and this was underscored by the rapt positive feelings shown by the leaders of the world.

Hanover Simpson leaned toward Bathsheba and the Ubies and toasted what he called "the signature moment of the past three months and I am so proud of being a small part of it," saying it with the sincerest look he could muster. All this attention, he thought would be good for his career - his career as a movie producer, more than a former President of the U.S. His fertile mind was already thinking about a docu-drama, maybe a TV mini-series on Premier Ubi and his people who fought for what is good and just in a world that puts the premium on greed and ego-centrism. What a bracing, inspirational movie it would be, he thought, and, of course, he would be a central figure in the story line. What could be more perfect?

After the drinks, they bade Joe adieu, got back in Simpson's long white limo and headed for the new Russian Tea Room on West 57th Street, where they, as Simpson knew would happen, received a standing ovation from the patrons as they walked through the bright red and Kelly green room to the banquette in the far back corner. Simpson couldn't be happier in this haven of show business and eccentricity. He was becoming all he really ever wanted to be and he was doing good deeds at the same time. What could be better?

❈

CHAPTER THIRTY-ONE

Critical Mistakes Are Made

P LATSY S CHMID MADE A MAD SCRAMBLE
down a back alley off Abdidli Street. He was headed toward
the Marriott and he was not a pleasant sight with the rain
coming down in torrents and mud and muck flowing from
every direction. He fell several times and was dirt-caked
and bloody, looking as if he had been in a rugby scrim that
was on the losing side.

Being a true E.H. Meris man it didn't take him much
thought to sneak out of the locked-in Ubi Club. He simply
paid a porter there $100 American and the guy let him out
in a laundry truck. When it stopped a block down the back
alley, Platsy squirted out and made the mad dash.

Getting in the Marriott would be another matter, since
everybody was either locked in or locked out by the Ubian
demonstrators.

At first he thought he might just join in the throng
encircling the Marriott and somehow try to slip in the building.

Instead, he noticed that a large part of the Ubians had shifted toward the front of the Marriott, because of the mudslides coming from the sloping hills behind it. He spotted a stepladder near a service entrance, a stepladder not unlike the one that was found near the hanging body of Artha Crowder the week before. He climbed atop a seven-foot high service deck, pulled up the ladder and found a window, which he crashed with the top of the ladder. In he went.

There were no Ubians at the back of the Marriott, so the sounds of crashing glass fell on deaf ears, save for Platsy, who was now in the building and was feeling quite full of himself.

The chorus lines of Ubians surrounding the Marriott had seriously diminished as more and more of the natives had been removed to seek shelter on higher grounds. As Smiley Watkins looked out the window from his 16th floor suite, he began to think the siege was finally going to be over.

In the suite with him were Cabby Thomas and their various associates. Cabby was not at all happy with the weather nor with the conditions he found himself under in the Marriott, where there was no air conditioning, no food, water and any form of communication with the outside world, notwithstanding the fact that he was ensconced in the building with the love of his life, the porno star Lachitcha Lasos.

"This whole deal sucks," he grimly said to Smiley Watkins. "I'm out of here for more reasons than one."

"Why, why, why?" asked Watkins. "Look out the window, can't you see that the Ubians are leaving? They're givin' up. Can't you see? We'll get our deal done, you betcha, and you'll be paid a lot of money upfront and more from your interest in the golf companies over the yares to come. Ol' Premier Ubi will take our deal and run. He has no other choice. Look, his people are giving up on him."

"Look, you silly fool, those people are not leaving because they're giving up. They are going up to the highlands for shelter. They know a hell of a lot more about this land than you do, asshole," Cabby said in his usual condescending tone. "And we're so close to sea level, you don't know what the hell is going to happen in this kind of storm."

As he said these words, there was a rapid knock on Smiley's door. The knocker was Platsy Schmid, who had climbed the 16 stories to Smiley's suite, which he knew well because of its proximity across the alcove from Sheryl Chan's, his recalcitrant lover, whom he couldn't wait to see after doing his business with Smiley.

Platsy entered the suite looking like a mud Michelin man, covered from head to toe in pudding-like cakes of wet earth. Cabby looked at him, and uttered, "Who the fuck are you, our Savior, here to take us to da promised land?" Then he turned to Smiley and said, "You are one bizarre dude, count me out of this simple-assed deal in a Texas minute, you fat termite."

Smiley cast his eyes to the floor, thinking with all of his money - most of it borrowed - he should have more respect, but resilient man that he is, he looked up and asked Platsy who he was.

"I am the research director of E.H. Meris," Platsy said smugly. "I have come here to recruit you, Smiley Watkins, to join vith us and Father Crosetti in a three-vay deal to split up Ubi. Vee'll re-name the country and call it something more romantic. The main thing is that vee vill send Premier Ubi on his vay and do vhat vee vant to do, each of us."

Suddenly, Smiley's puffy blue eyes sparkled. "Son, ah do like cuttin' deals. That's what I'm known for. 'Big Deal Smiley' they call me back home. Nobody likes a deal better than ol' Smiley. Ah knew we could reach some sort of compromise, that's what I told your boss, Mr. Gigli."

"Look it, here's the vay they have put this together, they being Gilly Gigli and Father Crosetti of the Holy See. I am the messenger on this one," said Platsy. "And, I think you are damned lucky to be a part of this." Platsy hated thinking of himself as a messenger of any kind, but he knew the way he looked he didn't have much credibility speaking as the strategic executive that he is.

Cabby moved toward the door, but Smiley grabbed him tightly by his muscular left forearm, stopping him harshly. "No, wait, you have to hare this out. You can't leave until you hare what he has to say.

"O.K., this is it," said Platsy Schmid, the research director who had been so on the rise at the E.H. Meris Co. "Vee all sort of split up the spoils. You can develop the land around the sea for your golf courses and hotels and homes, E.H. Meris vill get enough of the eefer forest to vork vith and vee vill be very happy vith the results. And the Church vill own the land, the land that they originally owned until the stupid Cardinal Reidy sold Ubi Ubi the 24 square miles 24 years ago. The Church vill lease the property to us both and take out 20 percent of the gross revenue, the same deal Crosetti offered Ubi Ubi two veeks ago, and the dumb shit didn't take. The leasehold vill be for 100 years and then our respective companies vill own the parcels that they have occupied. It's a good deal all the vay around. Vhat do you say, Mr. Vatkins?"

"Ah say I'm in!" said Smiley.

"And, I say I'm out!" said Cabby Thomas, bolting for the door, and just as he opened it, Sheryl Chan could be seen across the hall, leaving her suite with her wheeled suitcase.

Thomas kept going down the corridor, hurriedly on his way to pick up his flame, Lachitcha Lasos, to get out of the country. He knew the Ubians would let them go, and maybe if the weather quelled some they could grab a flight to Beijing and then another to the U.S.

Platsy saw Sheryl leaving and reared toward the hallway.

"Sheryl, Sheryl, vhere are you going?… You can't leave… Vait 'til I tell you vhat is happening. Vhere in like Flynt."

"The Holy See is convinced they vill vin the land case against Ubi Ubi in the vorld court in Geneva and they are villing to lease the land to our company for the next 100 years and ve'll be able to take over the eefer production. Vee have victory in our hands. You can't leave."

"Platsy, have you lost your mind and where have you been?" she asked. "You look like you were on the bottom of the stampede of bulls at Pomplona. I have made a decision and it is firm. I am leaving this building and I'm going to leave E.H. Meris as well. I've been doing a lot of thinking sitting here the last few days with nothing else to do. Everything that is E.H. Meris sickens me. You sicken me. I want out and I know the people downstairs will let me out. Those people don't deserve to go through what we're trying to put them through. This is pure and simple avarice on our part. I loathe this oppression more than you can ever imagine and will not be a part of it any longer. Smiley Watkins and that creep of creeps, Father Crosetti, are in the same boat with you and Meris. Think about it, this is the plain and simple truth. This is the difference between good and evil and I prefer to be a part of the former."

With that, Sheryl started down the hallway and then she would go on the long trek down 16 flights to the ground, clanking her heavy wheeled bag on each step.

Standing at the doorway of Smiley Watkins suite, the muddy, bloody Platsy Schmid, who doesn't give up easily obviously, could be heard to murmur, "Come back then, come back, Sheryl. Can't vee do it just one more time for fun? Please one more time?"

Sheryl continued down the hall to the stairwell exit, never looking back.

Platsy closed the door and looked forlorn. But in moments he was back to his usual self, telling Smiley Watkins, and Smiley's two assistants, Jay Weatherspoon, the executive vice president, and Harry Gerthperker, the head of finance, what a good deal this was going to be for everyone.

Suddenly, the door broke wide open. And in came Jimmy Christian, Dennis Columbus, Caz Caswell and Felonius Assault, and a few seconds later, Admiral Robert Peter Schnuck himself. They had rage on their faces.

"Get out, Get out of my suite? Who the hell do you think you are," yelled Smiley Watkins. "Get out of here, Get the hell out of here!"

"No, you're the one who is going to GET out of here," Admiral Schnuck shrieked. And he advanced forward, pointing his finger toward Smiley Watkins, Platsy Schmid and the others, but mostly at Smiley Watkins.

"Don't you point your finger toward me, ya tinhorn fake of an Admiral. You can't even save your little country for your little premier can you, asshole?" yelled Smiley. "I heard all about ya, Schnuck, yar the stupid fart who blew up yar own three cruisers in the Falkland Island crisis."

By now, Admiral Schnuck was furious, and continued to advance toward Smiley, who started to back up but still pointed back at Schnuck.

Now they were standing nose to nose, the six-foot-plus Schnuck somewhat staring down on the five-nine Watkins. Watkins made a tactical mistake when he thrust his right forefinger toward Schnuck's chest and it hit Schnuck. Schnuck pushed Watkins back with his own forefinger, and then Watkins did the same thing in return, though backing up. And Schnuck made one more thrust of his own, not belying his powerful strength. This one hit so hard that Smiley was pushed hard backward through the open French doors onto the balcony of his suite. Admiral Schnuck reared back again and landed another right forefinger to Smiley's chest and this one pushed him over the top of the balcony railing. Admiral Schnuck looked down and saw a big white snowball with black shoes and a red face squirting down to the ground below. The snowball landed right between eefer tree "A" and eefer tree "B."

While this was happening, Platsy Schmid tried to run from the suite, but Columbus, too quick for him, grabbed him by the neck and threw him to the floor. "You, you killed Artha Crowder, you son-of-a-bitch."

"I did not, I did not," came the words from Platsy's muffled-to- the-floor mouth.

"Yes, you did, and we can prove it," huffed Columbus, with Jimmy Christian standing over him, scowling.

"Let me in there! Let me in there! Let me give this rotten prick what he deserves," yelled Jimmy.

Dennis pushed Jimmy away and pulled Platsy from the floor. "We can prove you killed Artha for three convincing reasons. One, the teeth marks on one of the cigars found in Artha Crowder's coat pocket match the teeth marks on another cigar we retrieved from Sheryl Chan's room yesterday. We called on her to ask if you smoked Romeo y Julietta Cubans. She said you do, that she knew Augustino Crosetti gave some of them to you at the Ubi Club, because you bragged that he did. Our medical examiners checked the teeth marks and there is no mistake that they came from the same person. We are convinced that in trial you will be found guilty when the D.N.A. evidence is in as well.

"The other evidence against you is that you Velcroed Artha's tie to his shirt, his suitcoat to his trousers and his trousers to his socks, trying to make it look like a fastidious little suicide as he hung upside down from the first limb of eefer tree "A." We just found strips of the identical Velcro in your room here at the Marriott, cut almost to the same size as the strips found inside Artha's clothing.

"And one more thing, there was the scent of Chanel #5 on Artha. We know that you had been consorting with Sheryl Chan that same day. She told us about it and she said she wore Chanel #5, an unusual perfume for a young woman to wear. It has a strong aromatic scent and that smell poured right out with your sweat onto Artha's clothing."

"I did not kill him, I did not," sobbed Platsy Schmid. "I did not kill him."

"Well, maybe I can convince you that you did," exclaimed Jimmy Christian, whose piercing black eyes looked menacing and determined.

He then dragged Platsy by his ankles to the balcony and with the great power of his arms and shoulders, the former pro baseball player whipped the Swiss research director over the railing. "I am 63 years old, not as strong as I used to be, and I'll hold you out here as long as my strength will allow, or you can just tell us why you killed Artha."

Hanging by his ankles from the hands of Jimmy Christian, Platsy looked down from the 16th story balcony. He could see the white-suited body of Smiley Watkins on the ground. Not a pretty sight.

"Yeah, I bet you can see that big white turd ball down there. You can join him shortly, like a big mud ball. Hope my grip doesn't slip too soon."

The others looked on in amazement and some horror. They didn't move for fear that Jimmy would lose his grip. As he held Platsy out over the railing, Platsy's head would bob back and forth like a Swiss metronome, hitting the back of his head on the base of the balcony every second or two.

"Don't drop me… Don't drop me… I give in. Don't let me go. I'll tell you vhat happened. Please, please don't drop me," he sobbed.

Columbus reached forward to help Jimmy reel Platsy Schmid back in. When they did, Schmid fainted. And Jimmy gave him a hard slap to the cheek to wake him up.

The detective and the bar owner then threw Platsy on the bed, waiting for him to get the courage to spit out his confession.

Admiral Schnuck was in soft tears, as he thought about why this man would have killed his good colleague, Artha Crowder.

As if an omen, the skies outside appeared to be clearing some, and there was some faint sunlight. The winds had died down but it was still raining.

Jimmy Christian, perspiring profusely, held Platsy's chest down. "What in the hell did you do this for? What purpose did it serve? How could Artha have been a threat to you or hurt you or anyone else? He was simply the information minister for our country."

"I... I... I didn't mean to kill him," said Platsy. "He had come to my room to see if he could get to Gilly Gigli. Our CEO refused to see him, but I think he vas trying to determine if there vas some vay to resolve our disputes vith the Country of Ubi. I had come vith Genny Chancellor, who introduced Artha Crowder to me. Crowder vas very nervous but said he vanted to resolve the problems for Premier Ubi and get us all out of the country. I said vee veren't going anyvhere, and he threatened me and said if I didn't get him a meeting vith Gigli, I vouldn't be around to see tomorrow. I grabbed him by his lapels and threw him to the floor of my room. I vas going to hit him in the chops, but he vasn't moving. He vas out cold. I think he vas dead right there. I got scared. Vhen Genny saw that, he ran out of the room. I think he vent to see Father Crosetti. But I vas only doing this in self defense."

"Self defense, all right, self defense," said the detective Dennis Columbus. "You must weigh 40 pounds more than Artha Crowder. He was thin as a rail. You say he threatened you. He threatened you with what? We don't allow guns here in Ubi and I've never seen a hand knife. How did he threaten you?"

"He had a hand grenade and he said he vas going to oil it up and shove it up my arse. He showed it to me. I tried to knock it from his hand but he vouldn't let go. I didn't vant him to pull the pin and blow us both to bits. So I pushed him to the floor and he vas knocked out."

"You claim he had a grenade and he was going to kill you, but you instead killed him," shouted Jimmy Christian, still panting from having hung Platsy Schmid out to dry.

"When we checked your room for evidence this morning, we didn't find any grenade, just the Velcro strips you obviously cut to fake Artha's suicide," said Columbus. "The roll of Velcro where they came from was found inside your briefcase."

"He threatened to kill me and I had to take action," cried Platsy. "He vas going to blow me up, maybe himself vith me. He looked crazy and insane. I vas very scared. Vhat vould you do? Vhat vould you do? I thought I vas going to be killed."

"Well, you little punk, I sure as hell wouldn't have been scared about this," said Columbus. "We also found this in your hotel room, under the bed; apparently it had slipped out of Artha's hand. At that, Columbus pulled from his pocket, a rubber "Mr. Potato Head," very feebly looking like a hand grenade. Well, at least it was green. Also, it was one of Filigree the macaw's favorite toys. It squeaked like a gored pig when you squeezed it. And this was the threat to Platsy Schmid.

Jimmy Christian looked like he was going to take Schmid over the balcony again and drop him this time.

"The killing may have been by accident, we don't know," said Dennis Columbus. "But you are guilty of covering it up and taking a man who may not have been dead when you hanged him upside down, just unconscious. You made a fatal flaw when you stuck your own cigars in his pocket. Why did you do that?"

"Before he came to my room, I had been smoking the Romeo. I had several of them given to me by Father Crosetti one day vhen I saw him vith Genny Chancellor at the Ubi Club," said Platsy, sobbing even more now, his chest heaving. "I knew that this vould be a long night. I didn't know vhat I vould do vith him, but I knew I had to get him out of my room.

"I didn't have a jacket, so I put the cigars in his inside breast pocket for the time being, thinking I could smoke again once I completed vhat I needed to do vith him."

"Which was?" asked Columbus.

"Vell, I knew I must make this not look like the vorst. I thought a suicide vould do it. I knew he vas fastidious. Kind of foppish, if you ask me. Very eccentric. I figured if he vere to commit suicide by hanging, he vouldn't vant to look bad in the process. That's vhy I decided to Velcro everything.

"I pulled him out the door and down the hall," Platsy continued. "I dragged him into the service elevator and vhen vee got downstairs I vent out the back door. I saw the stepladder, and thought I vould tie him up by the ankles and I threw the rope over the first limb, pulled him up, and threw the ladder on the ground beneath him. He could have climbed the ladder and knocked it down and killed himself. It vas believable."

"Well let me say, Schmid, you, in fact, killed him, because the medical examiner, Dr. Habib, will testify that he wasn't dead at first," Columbus said scornfully. She says he died hours later, from a burst carotid artery. He would have lived if you weren't trying to protect your sweet Swiss ass.

"And I forgot my cigars," Platsy boo-hooed. "No one vould have known if I did not forget my cigars. No one."

CHAPTER THIRTY-TWO

The Weather Calms, Victory Seems Won

Jᴍᴍʏ Cʜʀɪsᴛɪᴀɴ, Dennis Columbus and Admiral Schnuck escorted Platsy Schmid down the stairs from the16th floor and then out the front door of the Ubi Marriott. Standing out there was Sheryl Chan. She was momentarily leaving on the jitney up into the hills where thousands of the Ubians were gathering, even though the salty air had returned almost to normal. Shif-Lee Ubi, the Premier's son and Interior Minister, had thought it best to move his people up into the highlands. He had not seen a very bad storm in his lifetime, but he heard about them in this land on the Yellow Sea, west of Korea and right below China. His father had told him of what could happen and his grandmother had witnessed the rages of foul weather, very vile and foul weather that occur in this very peaceable part of the world. Shif-Lee was determined to move all of the Ubians some miles up into the steep hills that some people would call mountains. The clutches of media people followed them.

Cabby Thomas and Lachitcha Lasos, among others from Cabby's and the late Smiley Watkins' groups, took advantage in the break in the weather and were able to get on planes out to Beijing and off to their various destinations. Many others staying at the Marriott and the Ubi Club had done so earlier, as they were easily released by the Ubians from the lock-in directed at the people from Meris, the Holy See priest/lawyers and the Texas development interests led by Smiley Watkins.

Back at the Ubi Club, Gilly Gigli and Father Augustino Crosetti and their lieges, including Bobbe Birstein and Genny Chancellor, were having a celebration. The weather was breaking, the Ubians were leaving and they thought they had victory at hand. They smoked cigars and were able to crack open some stored cases of Remy Martin to toast themselves. They looked out the tall, arched windows of the Club and saw fewer and fewer demonstrators. They had no communication with the outside world short of what they could perceive out the windows. But they felt they had dealt the winning hand against Premier Ubi and his 60,000 followers. They did not know that hundreds of millions of others from around the world were sitting in favor of the principles and causes of Premier Ubi. They thought they would surely win in the world courts in Geneva, win the right to Ubian land, and also win the approval from the World Health Organization to have the E.H. Meris Co. take over the global production of the eefer seeds for the multitude of medicinal purposes the seeds possess. They thought it wasn't much to let Smiley Watkins build his little Cancun along the shore, with the hotels, which were much needed, the homes, and, of course, the golf courses, which they could all enjoy in this distant land. They weren't aware that Smiley was out of the equation, nor that their executive messenger Platsy Schmid was under house arrest and being taken up to the highlands for the time being.

Some hours later, they were still celebrating, and by then all the Ubians, the media people and some other visitors had cleared out of Fung-Hi and moved up to the hills, protecting them like the Great Wall of China itself. They were protected from above as well by the canopy formed from the thickets of ancient vines, the last lines of eefer trees and assorted other full vegetation that was found in the highlands. Shif-Lee, Admiral Schnuck and their assistants felt that this was the smart thing to do. They just had a hunch the bad weather had not yet really subsided.

There was a stillness for several moments. Then the first clasp of thunder shook the walls of the Ubi Club. The second came immediately after. And a third. Lightning scattered in wild geometric directions in the skies. Another thunderbolt. More lightning and, then, a roar from out in the distance. And then an amplified chorus of "lions," frightening growling sounds from the sea, and growing louder and closer. The first heavy wave hit the jetty and blew it from its pylons. Another waved followed, maybe 20-feet high, and another 20-footer. Than the eeriest of all, a huge, thick, high wave rumbled from the distance and roared closer and closer to land. A ripping, twisting, constant avalanche of seawater moved inexorably forward. The sound was beyond the belief of anything the inhabitants still in the Ubi Club had ever heard. Father Crosetti looked out and saw the wall of water cascading rapidly toward the beach; he made the sign of the cross and looked down at Gilly Gigli still smoking a Cohiba Churchill, not fully appreciating what was happening, what with his Remy stupor going full bore.

The water wall hit the beach and just kept going, knocking everything in its sight to the ground, man-made edifices being torn to shards and shreds, concrete splitting like giant walnuts in a nutcracker. At the Ubi Club, the water had entered the building before totally taking the stoutly constructed granite structure to its foundation. The water started up into the fore-hills, rushing through the eefer forests, straight up and toward the highlands, going inland a good three miles, maybe four.

Up in the hills the Ubians crowded together along a trough formed by the south and north hills, the northern ones being along the Chinese border. They were scared but apparently safe from the Tsunami that had erupted beneath the Yellow Sea and had caused the tidal wave of a hundred feet in height.

And suddenly there was a kind of reverse roar, a retreating, sucking sound, as if the sea had taken a huge yawn and was retreating rapidly. Just as fast as it had come up, the tsunami wave went back. The sea reduced itself to a placidity and almost a flatness. The Ubians tried to peer out through the vegetation to see if it was yet safe for them to journey downward. Rains came down heavily, obscuring their view but they seemed to think the worst was over. And it was.

Some hours later, day was breaking, and some of the Ubians, led by Admiral Schnuck and Shif-Lee and their associates began trekking downward on foot. They couldn't believe their eyes.

Not one man-made edifice was left standing. In fact, not a sign of any of those buildings, bridges, piers or anything could be noted. Everything was swirling surreally in a grassy green, rainforest type of environment below. Nature had taken its toll, but down below the most amazing sight was that of the eefer trees standing tall and regally. Not one of them could be seen on the ground. Those who witnessed this sight first were rendered speechless. Everything they knew was lost, all possessions all marks of a civilized community. But also everything had been won. The eefer trees endured and so did the Ubian people, not one of whom, like the eefer trees, was lost.

As the lead crews, now in jeeps and jitneys got closer to the Fung Hi business center nothing, of course, was left standing, save for the lowest lying eefer trees. Eefer tree "A" and eefer tree "B."

Admiral Schnuck looked up to the first branch, some 10 or 12 feet above the ground. He looked up and he pointed at something, alerting Jimmy Christian, Shif-Lee, Caz Caswell, Felonius Assaut and Sheryl Chan, who were part of his group. And he asked, "Do you see what I see?" They did.

From the first branch, in the crotch between the trunk and the limb, could be seen a blue and white polka dot pocket square that belonged to Artha Crowder. It had not been Velcroed to his pocket by Platsy Schmid, like the other items of his apparel had been. It was the last vestige of the deceased Information Minister, strangely resting in the arm of the mother of all eefer trees, effer tree "A."

❋

CHAPTER THIRTY-THREE

Ubi Ubi Returns Home

THE GULFSTREAM JET LANDED at the Ubi International Airport one day later, the landing strips being the only remnant left of the airfield. Earlier, several of the large U.S. Army troop carriers had landed with supplies and tents to assist the Ubians temporarily with shelter. A veritable tent city was assembling to take care of the 60,000 inhabitants of the country. This was being accomplished quickly and fairly easily with the help of the soldiers.

Premier Ubi Ubi, his wife Taki, former President Hanover Simpson and his companion, Bathsheba Blakey, descended the stair door. The sky was azure and the sun smiled brightly upon them. Waves from the sea not far away from the airfield lapped lazily against the pink beaches.

Throngs of media crews crowded around the four. Premier Ubi ascended a makeshift stage set up with a portable amplification and speaker system from the Army. He addressed the media, but more importantly, his country people. Hanover Simpson looked on, beaming as only he could beam. He knew he'd be staying in a tent that night but, what they hey, he thought, he'd be in repose there with the lovely Bathsheba.

Admiral Schnuck peered up from below the stage and on his left shoulder sat the Ubies' macaw, Filigree, who as hard as it was for him to keep his beak closed, did not utter a sound as Ubi spoke. Like Admiral Schnuck, Filigree stood erect with an air of majesty. Jutting out of Admiral Schnuck's left breast pocket was the blue and white polka dot square that had belonged to Artha Crowder.

"This my fellow country men and women is the beginning of a new era for our land," he told the thousands. "Our eefer trees stand, as do we. Yes, we have a new beginning but we must never lose sight of the fact that this is a continuance of what our country and our principles have stood for for so long. We faced up to our oppression and we have won. The worst forces nature can bestow bombarded our eefer trees, and they stand.

"To all those looking in on us from around the world, I wish to offer our gratitude for your support and so too to the leaders of your countries who showed so much kindness when President Simpson and I visited the United Nations last week.

"It is time for our nations to repel special interests that have only their own goals at heart. There is a bigger picture for all of us as we seek peace and wellbeing for all of mankind.

"We of Ubi are blessed that we have the indigenous eefer trees on our land. These are trees that have given modern medicine some of its most dramatic cures in recent years and they promise to help us solve many other health problems in the future.

"We of Ubi pledge full cooperation in working with our pharmaceutical partners to achieve these goals for you and your loved ones as the 21st century continues. Even though the eefer trees were attacked by the worst storm to hit this land in a hundred years, they are left standing, and they will not miss one of their quarterly crops of eefer seeds used in medicines and herbs. We are all very fortunate for this. Just last week the World Health Organization, which had been in part manipulated by a giant pharmaceutical firm, realized it was being used, and ironically this week the W.H.O. announced five more distinctive remedies from the eefer seeds. These include treatments for asthma, plantar warts, epididymitis, trigeminal neuralgia, and sties. We now know of at least 100 effective treatments due to eefer, treatments medically benefiting and making life better for humans and animals."

"Bravo, bravo," screeched Filigree, the macaw, a bright bird that just might be smart enough to understand that the miracle of eefer could address the skin condition that left him with a luxuriant helmet of black and gold feathers but no feathers at all from the neck down.

The cameras whirred, microphones bobbed up and down and the thousands of Ubians applauded, recognizing Premier Ubi for his great leadership.

Then former U.S. President Simpson stood up to say a few words, if that were possible. He squeezed Bathsheba's hand as he headed for the lectern and nodded to Takita and Shif-Lee, sitting on the stage.

"Peoples of Ubi I want you to know what a great man your leader here is," said Hanover Simpson. "He is a leader of leaders. He has made such a lasting impression on me since we've gotten to know each other over the past several months that I am planning to make a motion picture about his life. To me, he is in a category reserved for the likes of Mother Theresa, Winston Churchill and George Washington Carver, Lou Gehrig and Mozart. One of a kind, whose principles and scruples are beyond reproach and to whom we must rejoice.

"My movie, which will be produced right after my earlier two films, 'Pirates Among Us' and 'Quebec City,' coming to a theater near you soon," he chuckled, "will center on a man from a nomadic existence who settled down to create his own version of 'Candide' for himself and all the people around him for the decades to come, only to be rebuffed by the worst forces mankind can conjure up. Premier Ubi built a country that all others should envy, a country without a judicial system, without lawyers if you can believe that, with no strong governing body. A country built on mutual trust for all who live there. A country that knows no racial strife or ethnic favoritism or prejudice.

"Premier Ubi himself is a collage of ethnicity. His father was Irish and Mongol and his mother Lithuanian. He could have settled for the touring life that had been the staple of his ancestral generations but at the age of 48 he decided to found your country, buying the land from the Catholic Church. As you know, the Church wanted the land back years later. The theory was Premier Ubi had acquired the land in a theoretically illegal or incomplete manner. But Ubi Ubi did not accept the dictum of the Church and fought for his land and his people.

"I am here to tell you today that I have received word that the Holy See has dropped all claims to the Ubian land and it has excoriated a group of its lawyers for acting too forcibly to execute those claims. My hat is off to the Holy See for seeing what is righteous for Premier Ubi, his family and all Ubians."

With those comments the crowd went wild with cheers. Hanover Simpson glowed. Ubi Ubi nodded with pleasure as he looked out at the sea of people. People watching on television from all corners of the world couldn't help but be tearful with joy, for they could see so clearly that the saga of the Ubians, fighting for their country in the most peaceful and genteel way, would end the way it must end. This was a profound story of David and Goliath proportions. The story of good, bad and evil and the forces of nature and human nature.

Admiral Robert Peter Schnuck, the de-commissioned officer of the Queen's Navy who had emerged in such a strong role in the saving of Ubi, looked up at his Premier with deep pride. Standing next to him was Jimmy Christian, a man whose talents allowed him to touch the outer edges of fame on the baseball field years ago but also one who would years later be part of the leadership to return his adopted country to its people.

Yes, there is a motion picture here, as Hanover Simpson is so determined to make. But nothing on the silver screen could properly depict the actual real-life drama that occurred in this country 24 miles square over the last few weeks.

As Hanover Simpson figuratively declared his hat off to the Holy See and the World Health Organization for determining the proper course of humanitarianism vis-à-vis the Country of Ubi, there was another hat off.

Not far from the airfield, not far from where the Ubi Club and the Ubi Marriott had stood just 48 hours earlier, near where the jetty once jutted bisecting the pink Ubian beach, a hat floated on the seawater. It was a Cossack black hat with red feather. It was the Cossack hat of Father Augustino Crosetti, the wretch of a priest/lawyer of the Holy See.

❋

Notes

Notes

Notes

Notes

Order additional copies
of this book!

You can order additional copies of *Dateline: Ubi* for your family and friends. You can easily order the book and get FREE shipping! You may:

Call 800-932-5420

or

visit www.airportbooks.com